Hot Taboo Erotica

Leighton's Odyssey

Casual
ENCOUNTERS

LEE NORTH

WARNING

This book contains sexually explicit scenes and adult language. It may be considered offensive to some readers. This book is for sale to adults ONLY.

* * * * * * * * * * * * * * * * * *

Please store your files wisely where they cannot be accessed by underage readers.

Please feel free to send me an email. Just know that these emails are filtered by my publisher. Good news is always welcome.

Lee North - **lee_north@awesomeauthors.org**

About the Publisher

4Fun Publishing, a member of **BLVNP Incorporated**, 340 S. Lemon #6200, Walnut CA 91789, info@blvnp.com / legal@blvnp.com
NOTE: Due to the highly emotional reaction of some people to works of erotic fiction, any email sent to the above address that contains foul language or religious references is automatically deleted by our anti-spam software and will not be seen. All other communications are welcome.

DISCLAIMER

Please don't be stupid and kill yourself. This book is a work of FICTION. Do not try any new sexual practice that you find in this book. It is fiction and not to be confused with reality. Neither the author nor the publisher or its associates assume any responsibility for any loss, injury, death or legal consequences resulting from acting on the contents in this book. Every character in this book is over 18 years of age. The author's opinions are not to be construed as the opinions of the publisher. The material in this book is for entertainment purposes ONLY. Enjoy.

Casual Encounters

Leighton's Odyssey

Hot Taboo Erotica

By: Lee North

© Lee North 2014
ISBN: 978-1-68030-131-1

Part 1 - Constance:

I could remember exactly when I knew my marriage to Jocelyn was over. It was the night of our tenth wedding anniversary. I came home early, brought flowers, and a nice silver pendant, that I knew she would wear. We kissed perfunctorily at the kitchen door, before I went upstairs to shower and change, prior to taking her out to her favorite restaurant for dinner.

What made it memorable is that we spoke hardly a word to each other, despite the fact that we had not seen or talked to each other since the previous evening. I typically left for work an hour before Jocelyn, and she was in the shower when I pulled out of the driveway that morning. At the restaurant, there were no reminiscences of past times together, no fond remembrances…nothing. We made the odd comment about the weather or our work, but nothing intimate. When we went to bed, I reached for her, hoping for at least some anniversary lovemaking, but she said she was too tired and that was that.

I lay on my back and knew then that it was over. We had each been pretending that our marriage was still alive. I thought back and realized, I wasn't even sure if we were ever in love with each other. We went through the motions, but I couldn't remember a moment when I knew for sure that I would do anything for her: walk through fire, slay dragons, or take on a gang of villains. It was a dispiriting thought, and with our life having sunk into ennui over the past two or three years, I knew a decision was at hand.

I delayed leaving for work the next morning. I might as well face it when I knew what I wanted to say. Jocelyn came down and was obviously surprised to see me sitting at the kitchen table with a coffee and the morning paper.

"What are you still doing here?" she asked, curious, as she poured her first coffee.

"I wanted to talk to you. It seemed like the best opportunity," I said quietly.

I suppose it was my tone of voice that alerted her. She looked at me, and then picked up her coffee, and sat in her usual chair.

"What did you want to talk about?" She was clearly uncomfortable with the uncertainty.

"Jocelyn, there's no easy way to say this. I will file for divorce early next week."

I watched her eyes grow large and heard the sharp intake of breath.

"Why?" she struggled to ask.

"I think you know the answer to that, as well as I do. Our marriage is dead. It died a long slow death, but it is dead," I said solemnly.

She sat silently, looking at me, thinking about what she had just heard. Slowly, she lowered her gaze to her untouched coffee, and stared at it for a few moments.

"I'm sorry, Lee. I wish it had worked. I'm sorry," she finally whispered.

"I know. Don't blame yourself. Sometimes ... sometimes it just doesn't ...." I couldn't finish the thought. I saw a tear, and then another trickle down her cheek.

"I'll look after the paperwork. If we use the do-it-yourself forms, we can cut the legal costs ... unless you want to contest it," I said, almost as an afterthought.

"No ... I won't fight it. You're right ... it just didn't come out the way we wanted it to."

I stood up, kissed her cheek, and left quietly for the garage and off to work.

If there is such a thing as an amicable divorce, we were the model. It was civil and civilized. We split everything almost 50-50. Jocelyn's income was very healthy as an assistant director in the provincial government Ministry of Environment. Thus, there would be no alimony. We agreed to sell the house and close the mortgage. Our home in Burnaby was valued at an almost ridiculous amount, after the eight plus years that we had owned it. After we retired the mortgage, we split nearly three hundred thousand dollars. We both had our own retirement savings plans, and maintained them in our own names.

Jocelyn kept her car, but I drove a company lease car with no asset value to me. I let Jocelyn keep most of the furniture, except for a couple of pieces that had come from my parents and grandparents. I guess, all told, she would have taken away thirty-thousand or so in value more than me, but in truth, I really didn't care. I just wanted the whole unhappy episode to be over.

We met once more, just before the divorce was final, to make sure that there were no outstanding issues to be resolved. We chose a pub not far from our former residence, and found a semi-secluded place to talk. It didn't take us long to determine that there was nothing left to discuss, except our feelings and our future.

"So, where are you going to live?" she finally asked.

"I don't know. I quit my job last week. I'll be finished at the end of the month, and then I'm going to do what the Aussies do; 'go walkabout.'"

"I almost envy you. I wouldn't mind a sabbatical myself. I hope you find what you're looking for," she said sincerely.

"Me too. I just hope I'll know it when I find it. What about you … where are you going to live?"

"I've taken a job in the Ministry of Industry and I'm moving to Victoria. I found an apartment there. I'll enjoy that, I think. Less pressure than Environment."

"Good … I'm glad," I said honestly.

"Regrets?" she asked.

"Sure. Plenty. I wonder if it would have turned out differently if I hadn't been sterile. I'm sure that must have hurt you more than you let on, finding out after we were married. I know it hurt me. Not good for the male ego."

"Yes … it hurt. But then, we talked about adoption and IVF. We had choices. I'm not sure that would have made a big difference except that maybe we might have hung on a lot longer because of the kids, and then become much more unhappy. Not much of a choice in my opinion."

"I suppose you're right. Well," I said, raising my mug, "here's to a better future for us. I wish you all the best, Jocelyn."

She touched her wine glass to my mug and offered a faint smile. A few minutes later, we hugged and kissed each other for the last time. I stood and watched, as she slowly worked her way out of the pub, and into the parking lot. I slumped back in my seat, waiting for the waitress to come around so that I could order another beer. I didn't have any place special to go, and I was in no hurry to get there.

I moved in with my folks for a couple of weeks after the sale of the house. They were very generous and sympathetic. Mom and Dad were married over forty years, and I think they were deeply disappointed at my divorce. I had failed at something important, and I think they knew that I was ashamed to admit it. They said nothing directly to me, but I could tell by some of their inferences what they were thinking. The sooner I hit the road, the better off they would be.

There was only another week until the end of the month and my employment. I think they were surprised and dubious about my unplanned future, but they said nothing to discourage me. On a bright and sunny Saturday morning of March, I loaded the last of my bags into my car, kissed and hugged my folks, and drove off into the sunrise. I had absolutely no idea where I was going, but I really wasn't worried about it.

I made the decision to explore my home province. At this time of the year, there was no need for reservations, since it was nearing the end of the ski season, and well ahead of summer vacations.

I drove for a couple of hours, stopping in Hope to stretch my legs, top up the tank, unload my morning coffee, and then get another fresh one at the kiosk, across from the gas station.

By noon I was in Keremeos, but I wasn't hungry and pushed on to Osoyoos, before stopping for a snack at a grocery store deli bar. On the spur of the moment, I decided to head for Nelson, a picturesque little town in the Kootenay Mountains. I would take my chances on a bed and breakfast, or in a motel, and if worse comes to worst, I could double back to Castlegar or Trail for accommodation. I pulled out my pocket guide to British Columbia B & Bs, chose one that looked likely, and thumbed the number into my cell phone. A mature sounding woman answered the phone and identified herself as Connie Bradshaw. I was in luck. She had a room and was featuring off-season rates.

It was almost six when I finally arrived in Nelson and found the Alpine Rest Lodge. I stepped through the outer entrance to the large, quaint Victorian house, and twisted the t-bar on the old fashioned ringer. In a matter of a few seconds, a woman appeared in the hallway and opened the door for me and ushered me in.

"I assume you are Mr. Stephenson?" she inquired.

"Yes ... Lee Stephenson. You must be Mrs. Bradshaw."

"It's Connie," she said smiling. "Do you not have any luggage?"

"In the car. I thought I'd check in first before I started to haul things in. I wasn't sure where I should park."

"Not a problem. Bring in what you need for your stay and park around the back. It's a reserved lot."

I filled out the registration and looked around the entrance, as Connie ran my credit card through. I was struck by just how elegant and detailed the old building was. It was in flawless condition inside, and I was anxious to see my room and more of the old house, if possible. I also took the time to survey Connie Bradshaw. She was somewhere in her late forties I guessed. Very attractive, with a still-youthful figure and a bright smile.

"You're my only guest tonight, Mr. Stephenson," she said as she handed me back my card.

"It's Lee. I was just admiring the interior of the house. It's very beautiful and in great condition."

"Yes, it has been a lot of work but well worth it. It was built by my great grandfather and it's been in the family ever since. I don't dare let it get rundown," she laughed.

"So you and Mr. Bradshaw are the keepers of the flame, then."

"No, just me. There is no Mr. Bradshaw." She said it with a smile and a slightly raised eyebrow.

"Oh ... excuse me. I didn't mean ...."

"That's quite all right," still with that enigmatic smile on her lips.

"Can you recommend a nice place for dinner?"

"Of course ... right here."

"Uh ... I was under the impression that this was a bed and breakfast," I said uncertainly.

"It is, but since you're my only guest and I hate to eat alone, you are welcome to join me."

"Well ... that would be very nice ... but I don't want to put you out."

"Nonsense … it would be my pleasure." She was obviously not going to take no for an answer.

"Perhaps I can find an off-license and supply a wine then."

"Why that would be very nice, Lee. I'd enjoy that. Make it a red … if that's all right with you." Her tone suggested that red was the only option. "There's a store connected to the pub on the next street up. It's less than a block, and you can walk there more quickly than you can drive."

"Great. Let me get my bag and you can show me my room," I said happily.

I picked my overnight bag and laptop out of the back seat, and followed the shapely backside of Connie Bradshaw up the stairs to the first landing. The sway of her hips was captivating, and I wondered if it wasn't a bit of a show for my benefit. If so, I was delighted, as well as somewhat stimulated. She unlocked the door and opened it, allowing me to enter first. It was as elegant and finely decorated as the rest of the house.

"I think you'll find this to your liking, Lee," she said again with that almost seductive smile. If I didn't know better, I would think she was at least flirting, if not actually hitting on me. I found that very pleasing. My ego needed a shot in the arm.

I set my bag down and checked out the ensuite bath, and found it to be correct for period and, as with the rest of the house, immaculate. I shook my head in admiration. Connie caught the gesture and smiled.

"I take it you're impressed."

"Very. I know something about what it takes to put an old house in this condition, and it isn't easy. This house is something special."

"Yes … it's my pride and joy. It's very unusual not to have several of the six rooms occupied, even at this time of the year."

She caught me staring at the big, wrought iron bed, and imagining what a romp in that big, queen sized pedestal would be like.

"That's a reproduction. I had it made locally to an old photograph from a family album," she explained. I suspected she was watching me and trying to read my thoughts. I turned to her and smiled.

"How about I go get that bottle of wine, and maybe we can enjoy a glass before dinner."

"An excellent idea, except I was going to make up a small shaker of martinis that we could share. I warn you, they are quite evil," she smirked.

"I haven't had an evil Martini in quite some time, if ever. I'll be right back."

There were some serious messages being sent to me, and I was becoming quite aware that Connie might have some designs on the entertainment portion of this evening. As I walked up the street toward the liquor store, I was surprised at just how blatant her moves were. She was not trying to be subtle. I thought about what the consequences might be, and considering my situation, I couldn't think of a single negative one. I decided that I would "go with the flow," and just see how things played out.

When I got back to the house, I used my key to enter the foyer just as Connie appeared. She was holding a tray with two shallow Martini glasses, and a small flask of premixed little devils that would probably do great harm if consumed in quantity. I offered her the bottle of French Cote d' Rhone, and she smiled her approval, again with the raised eyebrow.

"Come into the sitting room, Lee. We'll have our cocktails there before we move to the dining room."

I smiled in agreement, and followed her into yet again another impeccably finished space, with appropriate period furniture.

"I almost feel like I'm in a museum, a life size diorama," I marveled as I looked around.

"Well ... perhaps it is. Not everything is original. Much of the furniture has either been rebuilt, refinished, or a reproduction."

"It's very impressive. Very beautiful. I'm looking forward to seeing the outside in the daylight. Would it be alright to take some pictures?"

"Of course. I can use all the free advertising I can get," she chuckled.

She had a wonderful smile, and it made her more attractive than most middle-aged women. As I sipped my cocktail, I was appraising this impressive female. She was not slender; rather she was well proportioned, with what appeared to be fairly large breasts, and a definitely attractive hip flare that emphasized her delightful backside.

She must have been about five-foot-seven tall at least, but she carried herself as if she was still taller. She was wearing a simple print dress that seemed appropriate for the house, and yet displayed the fact that she was very attractive. She was an elegant woman, living in an elegant home.

We chatted as we enjoyed our Martinis. She was curious what I was doing by myself on the road, at this time of the year, if I wasn't in sales. I reluctantly told her of the dissolution of my marriage, and my decision to take some time off to recharge my batteries. I watched her reaction to my story, and she seemed to be both sympathetic and interested.

By the time we were ready for dinner, we had finished off the Martinis and I had opened the wine. Somehow, she had conjured up a wonderful meal of lasagna, caesar salad, foccacia bread, and the aforementioned Cote d' Rhone. By the time we had finished the meal, and were working on finishing off the wine, we had become good friends.

Connie wanted to know more about my marriage, and I have to admit that without the benefit of the martinis and the wine, I wouldn't have considered discussing my personal life with a woman I had only known for a little over two hours. But then, since my inhibitions were severely compromised, and I was alternating between lascivious thoughts about Connie and morose memories of Jocelyn, I spilled my guts out.

I'm not completely sure how it came about, but I found myself back in the drawing room with Connie sitting beside me on a love seat, listening intently as I tried to explain why I needed to take this time for myself. At some point, she'd put her arm around my shoulders and pulled me to her, making sure her generous breasts rubbed up against my shoulder and arm.

I was working very hard not to be downbeat, and to put a positive spin on my situation. I think that was the trigger for Connie. She was apparently turned on by my ability to look for positive, in a situation that others would consider a dark negative.

She was looking into my eyes intently, and I found that I had run out of things to say. I just sat there, looking back at this attractive woman, and I was about to look away when she leaned towards me and planted a lovely, warm, wet, and passionate kiss on my lips. There was even a hint of tongue. Her arm, still around my shoulder, pulled me into her and I couldn't help but put my arm around her, and allow my hand to travel up and down her lovely smooth back. My intelligence gathering foray, determined that she was wearing a narrow strap bra with a back hook. My high school skills had immediately kicked back in, as I sought out the zipper for her dress, establishing its location for future reference.

It turned out the future was now. Connie had moved her other hand to my crotch and had confirmed that I was harder than granite, and more aroused than I had been in months. As she slid her hand back and forth over my erection, I groped for her zipper and began to pull it down. As I leaned back to look into her eyes, I moved both my hands to her shoulders and pushed the dress off and down her lovely upper body. She was wearing a soft, champagne coloured bra that perfectly framed her beautiful, large breasts. There is no substitute for great tits, and this lady had award winners.

I was able to unhook the bra without a fuss, and I was gazing into her eyes as I slowly removed it. I could sense the fire inside her, and I guessed that it might have been just as long for her, as it had been for me since she'd had a good fucking. There is no substitute for alcohol when it comes to bravery, and I pressed my hands over her breasts and began to knead them softly, my thumbs quickly bringing her nipples to an enlarged state. I hadn't removed my gaze from her face since this had begun and she hadn't stopped looking into my eyes either. I leaned forward again and kissed her, slowly inserting my tongue between her lips. She opened her mouth, and we began to truly engage each other in mouth to mouth combat.

I knew by the erotic scent I had detected, that Connie was very aroused. I dropped one hand into her lap, and slipped it up under her dress and along her silken thigh. I discovered she was wearing 'thigh-highs,' and soon I was massaging her bare upper thighs, and slipping slowly towards her pussy. She had conveniently opened her legs to allow my advance, and as I touched the gusset of her panties with the edge of my hand, I could feel the dampness. The rest was inevitable.

The love seat was no place for a sexual union and we both knew it. I leaned back from her and asked, "Your place or mine?"

She smiled that lovely big smile and stood wordlessly, taking my hand, leading me to the back of the main floor. I followed willingly, knowing I was about to enjoy the favours of a wanton woman, who was undoubtedly a great deal more experienced than I. I was looking forward to it and was cautioning myself not to be too big in a hurry. I wanted this to be perfect for both of us.

Her bedroom was a larger and even more elegant version of my room, and I was led by her to another marvelous bed. She pulled back the coverlet and turned to me.

"Undress me, Lee," she requested in a soft voice.

"My pleasure." I pushed her dress down over her fulsome hips, and she stood before me in a pair of bikini panties, in the same champagne colour as her bra and the pale thigh-highs. It was a very erotic vision, and I moved to her and pulled her to me.

"You haven't finished yet," she said in a reproving voice.

"The panties go, the stockings stay." It was a moment of silly bravery by me.

She just smiled and I had apparently been given her approval. I began to remove my cotton pullover but Connie intervened and pushed my hands away. It was clear she wanted to undress me and I was fine with that. She undid my belt buckle and slipped my jeans down. She pulled off my boat shoes and socks before finishing the removal of my jeans.

So there we stood. My hands were back on her breasts and she was leaning into me with one hand on my erection. With a single move, she pulled my jockey shorts down and I was naked. My erection sprang forward and she seemed pleased with what she saw. I gently placed my thumbs in the waistband of her panties and slipped them down over her hips, letting them fall to her feet. She stepped out of them and took my hand, leading me towards the bed.

"You are a very beautiful woman, Connie," I said, meaning every word.

"Thank you. You're very handsome and I can see that you are definitely interested in me."

Her hand moved to my cock and she gripped it and began to squeeze it gently. I could feel the pre-cum leaking out of the glands, and I began to pray that I could hold out long enough to satisfy this very desirable woman. I reminded myself not to hurry and make sure I concentrated on her pleasure.

I pushed her gently back on her bed and placed my hands on each side of her hips. I leaned forward and began to lick and tease a breast, first the areola and then the nipple. She responded almost instantly and I could feel her back begin to arch. She was quickly aroused and as I switched to the other breast, I guessed that I would easily be able to bring this woman to orgasm. I played with her breasts with my tongue for a few minutes, and then I began to move southward. She flinched when my tongue entered her navel as I persisted in teasing her.

I continued my journey down toward her mons and my tongue traced the outlines of her labia. She twitched and reacted to my gentle strokes as I got closer and closer to her now very wet centre. Her scent was almost overpowering in its erotic aroma as I moved ever closer to her outer lips. As I touched them for the first time, Connie jerked in a spasm, and I heard her gasp as she reacted to this latest sensation.

I felt her hands on the back of my head and I recognized the meaning. I began to stroke her lips more forcefully and she began to pull my face more compellingly into her pussy. I hadn't yet touched her clitoris and I didn't intend to until I had achieved all I could from her slit. I moved my head down further and my tongue touched her perineum and she immediately reacted to that new sensation. I could hear her moaning now as she became either more aroused or more frustrated. I wanted to bring her to orgasm and I guessed that when I moved to her clit, it would be all over.

I pulled my head back to look up her body towards her. The lower part of her face was partially obscured by her breasts, but I could see that her eyes were almost closed and her head was rolling from side to side. I looked down at her bright pink pussy and I could see her clit was erect and it only took a single stroke of my tongue to have Connie erupt into a loud cry of surprise, as her hips rose violently from the bed toward my mouth. The second, third, and fourth strokes on the little nub were more than enough to produce her orgasm, and she was rigid with her glorious ass arched above the bed. She has very loudly proclaimed her pleasure.

"Oh Lee, oh Jesus … awwwwwh!"

It's a very satisfying sound to a man.

She collapsed on the bed and was breathing deeply as I moved up beside her. I reminded myself that I was in no rush and we were not limited by any time constraints. I lay beside her as she began to come down from what was a very explosive orgasm.

"Is Connie short for Constance?" I asked softly.

"Hmmm."

I took that as a yes.

"It's a name I've always loved. Something about it and the universe. The stars and the moon and the sun are always where they are supposed to be and they will be ten thousand years from now. Constance is a beautiful name for a beautiful woman. I would like to call you by that. May I?"

She turned her head and looked at me. It took a minute as she tried to decide if I was serious, but then she smiled. "I'd like that very much. It will be just for you, though," she cautioned.

We lay they for a few moments when she turned back to me. "Is Lee your formal first name?" she asked.

"Leighton ... Leighton Philip Stephenson."

"Oh, I like that name. Very distinguished. May I call you Leighton?" she asked seriously.

"Yes, of course. But only you and my mother," I laughed.

"Well, Leighton Philip Stephenson, are you going to finish what you started?" she asked with that sly smile and another arched eyebrow.

I rolled over on my side and began to stroke her body from breasts to thigh. I think she knew my answer. We kissed passionately again and my hand slid between her thighs and searched out her centre. She was no longer just damp, she was awash in her fluids. I needed no further encouragement as I mounted her. She spread her legs, bringing her knees up in a welcoming gesture and with no more than a single probe to locate her opening, I pushed slowly but firmly into her.

I was surprised with her tightness as she gasped at my invasion. I sank into her until our pubic bones touched and just stayed there for a moment. She was showing signs of becoming impatient and I could feel her muscles contracting as she tried to stir me into action. I pulled my head back and smiled at her, lowering to kiss her gently and then began to stroke, slowly at first, and then gaining pace. I was determined to make this last but Constance was not going to make it easy for me. She was gripping me with her vaginal muscles and she was pushing me further along.

"Constance ... if you keep doing that I'm going to finish before you want me to," I gasped.

"Don't worry ... I'll bring ... you back ... I promise," she promised between deep breaths.

It didn't matter. I was quickly losing control. I hadn't had passionate sex for so long I had forgotten how powerful a force it was. I finally surrendered and just let it all go.

"Awwwwwh ... Oh ... Connnn ... I'm going to ... finish." I was lost in the sexual whirlpool we had created. I came with a loud "agggghhhh!" and that was that.

I had no idea if she had come with me or at any time during my efforts. I don't ever recall having sex that even remotely resembled what I had experienced in the past few minutes. It had never been this intense.

"I'm sorry, Constance. I just couldn't wait any longer."

"It was your turn. Next time we share. You really did go off, though," she laughed.

"Yeah ... I did ... that was wild." I was still partially out of breath.

Constance had rolled on her side and one breast was lying against my chest while her fingertip was drawing patterns nearby on my abdomen. I took my fingertip and gently traced the outline of the areola and then the tip of her nipple. Her eyes closed and I felt her hips begin to move into me. She opened her eyes, smiled and then began to slide down my body.

She grasped my partial erection gently with her hand, and after looking into my eyes for a moment, bent her head to my manhood and began to kiss and lick and stroke and suck and generally make love to it. This was something that Jocelyn never wanted to do but that Constance certainly did. And she was good at it. Very good! I was rigid in a matter of a minute or two, and if I hadn't had such a major orgasm just a few minutes earlier, I would have come in no time at all. As it was, I could feel the stirrings in my groin and scrotum and I wanted to warn her.

"Constance ... if you ... keep doing that ...." It was the only warning I was capable of providing. I was torn between having the best blow job I had ever had or even hoped for, and my responsibility to my lover to complete her pleasure. What I didn't realize was that the experience and skill of Constance was at play, and she seemed to know just exactly how far to take me before backing off and letting me recover. She was amazing. She brought me to the edge three times and each time I was sure I would surrender and each time she kept me from falling off. Finally, she decided she had tortured me enough for the time being.

She rose and climbed up my body until she was straddling my face. She slowly lowered herself onto my mouth and I hungrily began to feast on her. I couldn't see anything as I licked and kissed and sucked and tickled, but I knew by her reactions that I was on the right track. Soon, she was bouncing all over the place and it was all I could do to keep my tongue and mouth on target. Finally, she mashed her sex down on my mouth, nearly loosening some front teeth with her pubic bone, and I heard her wail of approval.

She was still for a minute, on her hands and knees, and then began to move further forward off my face.

"Take me from behind, Leighton. Take me now!" she commanded.

I rolled over and propped myself up on my knees as I approached her from behind. I grasped her hips and pulled her back toward me to give her more room. In a single stroke, I quickly entered her and began to move into her forcefully.

"Harder ... faster ... do me Leighton! Do me hard!" she gasped her demands.

In seconds I was pounding into her at a furious rate. I knew I wouldn't last too long this way and I decided to slow for a minute or so to calm things down. She was having none of it.

"No ... don't you dare. Fuck me Leighton! Hard! Now!" There was no compromise here.

I resumed my frantic pace, and I was getting closer to the finish with each pounding stroke. Somehow or other I managed to last long enough to sense her change in response and the beginnings of what I was sure was her orgasm. I prayed to the gods that I could last long enough to give her what she so richly deserved, and the gods answered me kindly.

"Ahhhh ... fuck ... that's perfect ... that's so perfect ... ahhhh!" she squealed in an almost little girl voice. As she voiced her orgasm, her vaginal muscles gripped me tightly and it was all over for me. I came with a series of grunts and a final groan as I pulled her lovely ass tightly to my groin. I stayed there motionless as I felt my erection diminish and after a while, it finally slipped out of her. She had been gasping for breath and turned her head to look at me.

She had a big smile on her face and her eyes sparkled as the sweat dripped off her forehead. "Nicely done, Mister. What did you say your name was?"

I burst out laughing and fell over on my side and she fell with me. I nearly fell off the bed but Constance saved me and we held each other, laughing as we came down from our high. She had reminded me that sex could be fun as well as exciting.

"I hope m'lady found my performance satisfactory?" I said with as serious a tone as I could manage.

"Oh, me thinks t'will do," she grinned back at me.

I lay there for a minute just studying her and thinking about what had just happened. I could see the clock radio on the other side of her body, and it read 10:18 pm. I had met this woman a mere four hours ago, and here we were in her bed, in this magnificent house, and I just had the best sex I could ever remember. What the hell was going on?

"Do you always treat your guests this well?" I asked cheekily.

"Of course. It's the best way to get repeat business." She couldn't keep from giggling.

"I'll bet it is." I leaned forward and kissed her gently and she returned it with the same soft touch.

"Where are you going tomorrow?" she finally asked.

"I don't know. I have no plan. I'm just moving along from place to place until I find something."

"Stay … stay with me. There won't be anyone here tomorrow or the next day as far as I know. We can continue this lovely little tryst at our leisure." She wasn't pleading, but she was serious. "You haven't seen the town yet. There's a lot to see and my rates for your second and third night are very reasonable." I couldn't fail to catch the real meaning.

"All right … as long as I'm not imposing on you."

"Leighton … you are a breath of fresh air. I haven't had a man in my bed in quite a while, and I don't know if I've ever had anyone, that I've had quite as much pleasure with as you. You make me feel young again." I could see that she was offering a very honest expression of her feelings.

I smiled. "You are young. You act and think young. I can honestly say that not for one second had I given any thought to your age. I was too busy trying to keep up with you."

"That's a lovely thing to say and it's a lovely thing to hear. Thank you Leighton." I thought for a moment, I saw a tear forming in the corner of her eye. I pulled her to me again and kissed her.

"Constance, this bed is a little messed up and a bit damp in places. Why don't we go up to my room?"

"How thoughtful. Do you mind waking up with a strange woman in your bed?"

"We are hardly strangers any more, and I always prefer to wake up with a beautiful woman in my bed. There is nothing more erotic than the scent of a woman when I wake. If it could be captured, it would be the world's first genuine aphrodisiac."

"Did your ex-wife know you had these special talents all bottled up inside you?" she asked playfully.

"No … I guess not. But then … well … she's not around any more and I have something much more exotic lying right beside me."

"Silly girl. She'll never know what she's missing out on."

"Why don't we agree we don't talk about her?" I asked carefully. "I'm here with you and you're the only one that matters. There isn't anyone else."

"I'm sorry. I didn't mean to open an old wound. That was thoughtless of me."

"No apology necessary. I'd forgotten what it was like to have truly uninhibited sex, if I ever even knew. It was fun as well as exciting. I really needed that and you were here to make it happen. I loved every second of it."

"I'm glad. I meant it when I said you were good for me."

"Shall we have another glass of wine? I can always run up to the store for another bottle," I volunteered.

"I have some brandy. Why don't we have that? It may help us restore some of our energy," she said in her sexiest voice.

"That sounds splendid. Shall I dress for the occasion?" I asked in a cheeky faux English accent.

She laughed a genuine laugh, and hugged me as I rose from the bed. She walked to the closet and came back with a navy blue terrycloth dressing gown which she handed me. She wore a black satin one which showed off her lovely legs and on occasion, the lower part of her finely sculpted ass. Her breasts swayed languidly under the smooth fabric and I could see the nipples become erect once more. It looked to me like we were going to be making just as big of a mess on my bed, as we had on hers. Oh well.

I awoke the next morning with the sun streaming through the light fabric curtains, and lighting up the entire room in a lovely pastel yellow shade. Next to me Constance is asleep, and I moved my head towards her shoulder to sample that marvelous sexual aroma a woman produces in her sleep. It was intoxicating and stimulating. I had an erection but I also had a full bladder. I slipped out of the bed as carefully as I could without waking her, and then nearly blew it all when I stumbled over the dressing gown that lay in a heap on the floor beside the bed.

I crept as quietly as the floor boards would allow, and softly shut the bathroom door behind me. I must have had quite a full bladder, because I thought the stream was never going to end and the sound might have wakened the dead. It's always difficult when you're trying to pee with an erection, and this was no exception.

As I stood there, I thought about the last twelve hours. Constance was as real as the bed and our nakedness. This hadn't been some extended wet dream brought on by a porn movie fantasy. I had actually gone to bed with a beautiful older woman, made love to her several times, and awoken this morning with her sleeping peacefully beside me. If this was a dream, it was one of my best ever.

I had noticed my overnight bag on the floor, exactly where I put it when I had first seen the room. I wanted to brush my teeth and shave and probably shower, but to do that, I needed to get into my bag. I quietly opened the door to find Constance propped up in bed, the sheet draped around her waist, and a smile on her face. I winked at her and walked naked and somewhat self-consciously towards her.

"Good morning," I said as I sat facing her on the side of the bed. My hands went to her lovely large breasts and I fondled them as I gazed into her eyes.

"Good morning, Leighton. Did you sleep well?" she asked, wrapping her arms around my neck.

"Wonderfully well … except for the erotic dreams. They were very stimulating," I said softly.

As she nuzzled her lips into my neck she whispered, "Tell me about your dreams."

"I dreamt that I met this wonderful woman and she plied me with evil Martinis and wonderful food and then seduced me. It was very … exciting."

"When she seduced you, what did she make you do?" she asked, smirking.

"Why, it would probably be easier if I showed you." And so I did.

She tasted as wonderful that morning as she had the night before. She responded just as dynamically as she had the night before. Our pace was a little slower, and less frantic than it had been the night before. Her orgasms were just as enthusiastic as the night before. I was just as excited as I was the night before. We loved, and laughed, and stretched, and changed positions ,and generally made a complete mess of my bed, just as we had of hers the night before. It was wonderful.

After we had made love, I had been ordered to the shower and I used the time to shave and brush my teeth. When Constance finally rose, she went downstairs to her bathroom and I took the opportunity to explore the kitchen and its supplies. I surprised her by making the breakfast while she was in the shower. I found the necessary ingredients and by the time Constance had emerged from her bedroom, the scrambled eggs were in their final stages, the toast was made and in the warming drawer, sliced tomatoes fried, mushrooms sautéed in the skillet, and the coffee had finished its percolation.

She walked up to me and wrapped her arms around me, and pulled me to her for a passionate kiss. "I may just keep you here forever," she said with a smile.

"I might just stay."

She was wearing a pair of tight fitting jeans and a cotton pullover. As she moved near me, I suspected she wasn't wearing a bra. I ran my hands up the sides of her torso until I reached those lovely globes, and my thumbs extended to graze her nipples. She smiled as she realized what I was doing.

"You're trying to tempt me, aren't you?" I said with a sly grin.

"Too late for that, isn't it? Besides, I just like the freedom, and I know you like the look and feel, so why not?" she asked simply.

"No good reason I can think of." I kissed her and then led her to the kitchen table and pulled out a chair for her. She sat and I served.

"Leighton, these eggs are marvelous. What did you do to them?" she asked in genuine appreciation.

"Little simple formula involving Worcestershire sauce, a touch of chili sauce, and shredded sharp cheddar cheese."

"You'll have to show me. My patrons will go crazy for them."

We spent the rest of the day together. Constance was my tour guide for the delightful town of Nelson, and I was doubly lucky I had chosen that particular town and that particular B & B. My spirits were better than they had been in a long, long time. We visited a specialty wine shop and picked up several bottles of reds from France, Spain, and South Africa. Constance knew her wines and I was happy to be the carrier. I offered to pay for them, but she vehemently refused. She could be very strong-willed.

We lunched at a little deli near the far end of town, and I had brought my digital camera to take some photos of the many wonderful old buildings. We worked our way back to her home by mid afternoon and she checked the voice mail to see if there had been any last minute bookings. There had been none.

"Ah … I have you all to myself again," she grinned.

I turned to her and took her hand, pulling her to me. "Is this going to be another two bed night?" I asked, giving her a raised eyebrow.

"Probably. If you're … up for it."

"As long as you're with me, I'll find a way to be up for it."

"Hmmm … just what I wanted to hear."

I stayed with Constance for four nights. They were the best four nights I had ever had, and I would remember them always. By Tuesday night, I could tell it was time to go. Our lovemaking was still very passionate and fulfilling, but she would be welcoming guests on Wednesday and it would be awkward to continue our affair in those circumstances. I also suspected she was a little sore from all our activity.

Our lovemaking on Wednesday morning was sublime. It was gentle, and passionate, and calming, and immensely satisfying. We both knew that this was the end of this part of our lives, and we also knew we wouldn't easily forget these four days. We showered together, made breakfast, and ate together. In a few minutes, I had packed my small overnighter and was ready to leave.

She passed me a receipt for my stay and it showed only the one night that I had arrived. I looked at her in surprise and she put a forefinger against my lips.

"My treat, love. For services rendered."

I kissed her, wished her well, and promised to stay in touch. She had taught me a great deal and brought me a long way back along the path of restoration. She gave me a feeling of hope and had rebuilt much of my battered ego. She was a therapist of a very different kind, and only by chance had I stumbled into her life.

Part 2 – Glynnis:

I drove my Subaru Outback south to the edge of Nelson, stopping at the Chevron station. I topped up the tank, went inside to get a coffee, and returned to my car. I pulled out my B.C. map and looked at my options. If I really wanted to go north, I was better off to go south and then east. That's the way it was in the Selkirk's, the Purcell's, or any of the other mountain ranges in the Rockies for that matter. I always did want to run up the Rocky Mountain Trench, and this was a good time as any.

I thought back over the past four days and smiled to myself. Out of the blue and through pure dumb luck, I had met Constance and had spent the entire time in a state of sexual bliss. She had been a tonic of unimagined strength, despite our fifteen years of age difference. I kept thinking of the movie "In Praise of Older Women," and adding an *Amen* to the title. She was staring right at her fiftieth birthday, and yet acted more like a thirty year old playmate. In those idyllic four days, I had learned and experienced more in giving and receiving sexual satisfaction, than I had in my entire adult life.

I'm sure that anyone who saw me would immediately recognize the smug smile of a sated man. If I was going to die, this was the way I wanted to go. I sat in my car lost in my reverie, wondering how I would top this first adventure in my new-found freedom. The impatient blast of a horn was enough to get me going again, and I pulled out onto Highway 6, southbound to the Crowsnest, Highway 3 east. I thought briefly about continuing south into Idaho, but decided that side trip could wait for another day. I had my own territory to explore, and that's what I planned to do.

I was barely over an hour into my drive along the Crowsnest Highway and just approaching Cranbrook, when I felt something odd with the handling on the car. I had been cruising along at a sedate 90 kph when it began, and within a minute or two, I was aware that something was seriously wrong. I found a wide shoulder and pulled over to the side carefully, bringing the car to a stop. I got out and carefully looked at the wheels on the driver's side, before walking around the rear of the car to survey the passenger side.

The problem was obvious -- a nearly flat right rear tire. I had picked up a puncture, and after swearing at the inconvenience, I opened the rear hatch, took out the three bags that blocked access to my spare, and began my work.

When I had finished my last day of work, I had turned in my company car and purchased a two year-old Subaru from a dealer. I had the car checked out thoroughly by my friend and mechanic-neighbor Don Childs, and he pronounced it fit. He also gave me an 18" square piece of ¾" plywood to use if I had to change a tire on soft ground. I made a mental note to thank him with something tangible, as it was exactly what was required on this highway shoulder.

I wasn't likely to be recruited by any NASCAR team for my tire changing skills, but with the clever and efficient system Subaru and most other Japanese made had in storing and organizing the tools, I was done in less than fifteen minutes. I had a pair of leather work gloves in with the plywood platform, and I managed not to get too dirty with the effort. Luckily, the weather was nice and I wasn't under any stress, so when all was said and done, I wasn't in a bad mood at all.

It was only a few kilometers to Cranbrook, and as I arrive in the town, I began looking for either a Subaru dealer (unlikely) or a Yokohama Tire dealer. I found the latter first and pulled into a parking slot in front of the main showroom doors. As I approach the front desk I was greeted by an attractive young lady in light blue coveralls and the name Glynnis stitched above her breast pocket.

"Good morning. How can I help you?" she smiled.

"Good morning … Glynnis. I have a flat that needs repair," I said, examining her casually.

"Well, why don't I get one of our guys to bring it in and we'll get to work on it. It shouldn't take too long … it isn't busy this morning." She had a lovely smile and I've always been a sucker for nice smiles. Even when I'm angry or stressed, a nice smile can bring me down to earth in a hurry.

"Thanks." I continued to assess what might be under the coveralls. Damn … Constance had really changed my outlook on women in a hurry.

I helped myself to a hot coffee, although I think it had been made a couple of days earlier. I found a year old car magazine with an article on the Subaru Impreza WRX and settled in to wait for the tire repair. I had been there for about twenty minutes when an older man came through the shop doors, saw me sitting in the little lounge, and approached me.

"Are you the owner of the Outback?" he asked in a friendly manner.

"Yes."

"I'm afraid I'm not going to be able to repair your tire. It's been badly cut by some piece of metal I think, and I don't have any way to fix that. You're going to need a new tire. I can show you if you like."

"Sure ... let's have a look." It wasn't that I didn't trust him, but I was curious what would cause this kind of damage.

He showed me the inside of the tire and he had chalked an area about three inches long on a diagonal at the very bottom of the sidewall.

"I'm guessing you picked up a metal shard somewhere and maybe you rubbed up against a curb or something that pushed it through. Once the tire got hot on the highway, it would start to leak and deflate."

"Well, do you have a replacement tire?"

"No ... that's the thing. These aren't the standard factory tires. These are high performance touring tires and I don't carry them here. No call for them. Let me check the computer and see where I can get one."

We walked back to the desk and he started to enter keystrokes and within five minutes he had the bad news.

"The closest one I can find is in Maple Ridge. There's one in Edmonton too, but if I can catch the Greyhound, I can get the tire from Maple Ridge on the bus and it'll be here late tomorrow afternoon. That's the best I can do," he said apologetically.

"Well, luckily for me, I'm in no hurry, so why don't you order the tire and I'll just keep the car for around town until it arrives."

"Fine. I'll put the spare back ... no ... wait ... I think I've got a tire that's the same size in the bin. It'll do for a day or two as long as you don't try anything fancy with it. I'll put that on and you won't have as much imbalance as with that compact spare."

"That sounds great ... thanks a lot," I said genuinely. Small town service ... there's nothing like it. I left him my card and told him only the cell phone number was active. I asked him if he wanted an imprint of my Visa, but he said he'd sort it out when we finish putting the new tire on tomorrow. Small town trust to go with the service. I felt good about staying here for a day or so.

I had my car back in ten more minutes and he promised to call me when the new tire arrives and he'd put it on right away. Out of the corner of my eye, I could see Glynnis watching this interaction and she was smiling. I was about to walk out the door and get into my car when it dawned on me that I would be staying overnight in Cranbrook, but I had no idea where. In a moment of desperation, I turned back to the counter.

"Excuse me, Glynnis. It looks like I'm going to be staying overnight. Can you suggest a Bed and Breakfast or even a motel that would be comfortable?" I flashed my best smile and I got one in return.

"Sure. Mr. and Mrs. Straker have a very nice place in the west end of town. You probably passed along it when you drove in. It's a big yellow house with two big trees right in front. Would you like me to give them a call and see if they have a room?"

"That would be very nice. Thank you Glynnis." Again, I gave her the 100 watt smile. "By the way, my name's Lee Stephenson."

"My pleasure and it's nice to meet you Lee," she said with an interested look.

She quickly determined that there was room at the Straker's and in a simple photocopied map, she showed me where it was. I had indeed passed along it on the way to town, but I guess I was preoccupied with finding a tire repair location and wasn't paying much attention to the surroundings.

"You'll like their place. You can come and go without disturbing them. If you want to go clubbing tonight, you don't have to worry what time you'd get back." She said all this with a slightly wily look that began to give me ideas. Not totally wholesome ideas, either.

"If I want to go clubbing, where would I go?" I asked innocently enough to bring on another grin from her.

"Well ... there's a dance and drink club not far from here."

"So ... what's the dress code?"

"Nothing special. You get a real mix in a town like Cranbrook. Just don't wear a suit or a tie," she grinned

I laughed. "Well, I don't think that's a problem."

"It's called the Crowsnest Club. It's just down the street and it's the place to go for some fun, dancing, and a few drinks." She wasn't volunteering that she would be there, but I wouldn't be surprised if she was. I would make it a point to have a look tonight.

"Well, you've been a real help, Glynnis. I'd like to repay you for your hospitality. Are you doing anything for dinner tonight?" I asked, leaning on the counter directly in front of her.

She was obviously caught off guard. She wasn't expecting me to be so direct in asking her out, I guess.

"Not so far. What do you have in mind?" All pretence at mild flirting had disappeared and we were down to serious negotiation.

"You know of a nice restaurant I could take a good looking woman to?"

"Well … depends on what you like. Around here it's Italian and Chinese and steaks. Which do you prefer?" she challenged.

"Any of those sounds great. How about Italian?" I suggested.

"Florio's is very nice and quiet too. How does seven sound?"

"Perfect. Where can I pick you up?"

"I'll meet you there. That way, if you get too frisky, I can cut out," she laughed.

"A wise precaution. I wouldn't trust me either. Since you suggested the club, why don't we make a night of it?"

"We'll see. You don't look too dangerous, but you never know." She had taken more than a couple of seconds to agree, but I had the sense that she was looking for fun and I was it for this evening.

As I look at her more carefully, I guess she was mid-twenties, no more than five foot tall, with honest blonde hair, and an outdoor lightly tanned complexion. Her most outstanding features, however, were a class "A" set of breasts, and a very round and fully packed backside. She was a very sexy looking young lady, and I counted myself lucky that I was going to have the chance to spend some time with her.

I headed out to Straker's B & B and checked in. It was a conventional residence with a walk-out lower floor that was set up for three decent sized bedrooms, each with a small ensuite. I looked over it and decided it would be fine for the one or two nights I would be here. There was a small shower stall in the bathroom and a writing desk in the bedroom area. A TV and a clock radio on a nightstand were the only other items.

I unpacked and changed into fresh clothes and set up my laptop. I was surprised that the house was equipped with wireless, and I logged on without problem. I checked for emails and found none other than the usual SPAM and trivial stuff various friends had sent me. I had only been gone five days, so I didn't expect any emergencies. Besides, I had my cell phone, so anyone could find me if they had the number.

I left the room and drove back into town. I hadn't eaten since Constance and I had shared breakfast and I was hungry. I found a small store-front deli and decided to try it out. It turned out to be a good choice. The food was original, funky, and damn good. I thought some more about Glynnis and smiled to myself. My new freedom had produced two unexpected females in my life, and I was enjoying every moment of it. Constance had given me a good dose of self confidence and I was riding that high for all it was worth.

After I had eaten, I drove around the area using the simple map that Glynnis had provided. I saw most of the town, locating both the Crowsnest Club and Florio's Restaurant. Neither was more than five minutes from anywhere. In the summer, I would probably have chosen to walk to either of them. I thought about that for tonight if I happened to have a couple more drinks than I thought I should. I liked the idea of small towns and the closeness of everything. Cranbrook was bigger than average, but not so much that it lost that special feel these towns have.

I parked the car next to Florio's and walked around looking around the various shops on the streets nearby. I spent an hour in a book store and bought a couple of future readers for my travels. I found myself thinking a great deal about Glynnis, and what I was going to do tonight. My libido had been rekindled by Constance, and I was anxious to try out my seductive skills, assuming I had any. Glynnis had been very quick to accept my invitation to dinner and then to the club, and that was a bit surprising. I wondered what her story would be. I thought the best time to find out would be during dinner.

I walked into Florio's at five before seven and was seated immediately. I let the young lady at the front know I was expecting someone. Glynnis arrived just a couple of minutes after I was seated and I was pleased. It told me she was happy to be joining me this evening.

"Hi … good to see you again," I said, rising to hold her chair.

"Thank you. I'm glad you invited me. I like this place, and I wanted to get to know you a little better," she said candidly.

She was dressed in a short denim skirt and a peasant blouse with a nice expanse of cleavage. It was very much in a casual western style except for the shoes. They were at least three inch platform heels in gold fleck on black and she was all in all, showing a very sexy look. I wasn't sure about a bra, but it seemed like there was a lot of action going on under that blouse as she had walked to our table.

"Glynnis, I don't know your last name."

She gave me a funny look before she answered. "It's Florio," she said with a smile.

"Awww!" I had to laugh. "I suppose your parents are keeping an eye on you tonight?"

"Probably … but they know I'm an adult. I make my own friends and live my own life. They understand that," she said in a carefree tone.

"Hmmmm. My experience tells me that parents never quit watching out for their kids, no matter how old they are."

"Yeah … you're right. But mine are pretty good. I know they want me to get married and have a bunch of kids, but I'm still waiting for Mr. Right," she said seriously. "What about you?"

"Ah … well … I was married but … it didn't work out."

"Oh … I'm sorry. I didn't mean to pry."

"Well, sometimes things don't turn out the way you expect. We didn't have any children, so no real harm was done."

"I'm not so sure about that. I think when you're with someone for a while, it can't be easy to let go." It was a very thoughtful remark.

"No … you're right. It isn't painless. Luckily, we both recognized it wasn't going to last, so it made it a bit easier to put an end to the misery."

"I guess that's what I'm trying to avoid … I mean … picking the wrong one."

There was an awkward pause as the waitress took our drinks order and we looked at the menu for the first time.

"I don't know why I'm looking at this. I know it by heart," she said with a light laugh.

"What's the specialty of the house?" I asked.

"Osso Bucco," she said quickly. "Trust me, it is the best!"

I snapped the menu shut. "Great ... decision made."

The smile she gave me was infectious. I was enjoying myself again in the presence of a woman I'd only just met. "So Glynnis, am I going to have to learn to Line Dance tonight?"

She laughed out loud. "No! No! Not the dreaded Line Dance!" she spewed, almost choking on her drink. "We don't allow that kind of stuff on this side of the mountains. That's for flatlanders. I like slow, close dancing. Real slow and real close," she murmured suggestively, fluttering her eyelids.

Now it was my turn to laugh out loud. "You are a tease, young lady. Do your parents know about your naughty ways?"

"Nope. It's my naughty little secret."

The dinner was lovely and as advertised, the Osso Bucco was very good. We chatted about ourselves a fair amount. I learned that she was the "brains" of the tire store and that the older man that had looked after my tire problem was her uncle. Glynnis did the books and set up the computer systems for him. She enjoyed her work but hinted that she had a longer term plan in mind. She didn't spell it out, but I gathered it involved a guy she knew.

We lingered over a glass of wine and passed on the desserts. There seemed to be a bit of tension between us.

"Are you staying another night?" Glynnis finally asked.

"Yeah ... I think so. Sounds like the tire won't be here until late tomorrow, so there's no point in heading off. I'm in no hurry and I don't have to be anywhere special."

"Then, why don't we skip the club until tomorrow night. It's always livelier on Thursdays," she suggested.

"What would you rather do?"

"Hang out with you. Why don't we go back to your place? We can watch TV ... or something," she whispered with that sly grin once more planted on her face.

I gave her a knowing smile and agreed. "Okay ... let's go. I'll meet you there."

I had figured out that I was the only guest at the Straker's that night and with the private entrance, no one would know I had a guest in my room unless they saw us arrive. I had barely opened the door to my room when Glynnis arrived and whooshed into the room ahead of me. She turned to me as I closed the door and marched straight into my arms. It took me less than five seconds to determine that she was both horny and bra-less.

I'm a shade less than six foot, and Glynnis was a shade over five foot, so there was quite a height difference between us. One thing was certain, her nipples were rock hard and if I had hugged her any harder, I would have a pair of small bruises on my rib cage. I locked my hands under her lovely ass and hoisted her up to eye level. She wrapped her arms around my neck and I pushed her up against the wall and began to assault her mouth with my tongue. She was very active and very aroused and I finally walked her to my bed and dropped her as gently as I could upon it.

She lay there looking up at me and smiling like the Mona Lisa. What did she know that I didn't know, I wondered. I started to pull the arms of her blouse down over her shoulders and she wriggled her upper body to help move the blouse down. At the same time, she set in motion those lovely big orbs, and I was temporarily mesmerized as her shimmy made them dance inches from my face. I couldn't resist. I went after them with my mouth.

She didn't make it hard for me to capture one and I feasted on it, licking and sucking and nipping as she quietly moaned her approval. I changed sides to make sure I gave them both equal attention. As I watched them flow from one side of her chest to the other, a strange memory crept into my consciousness. A brief porn clip in the internet of a blonde woman with large breasts making them orbit in tandem while she was being fucked. It didn't look deliberate, but it was very erotic. I wondered if I could make that happen with Glynnis. It was worth a try.

I stood up and began to remove my shirt as Glynnis kicked off her shoes and undid the button on her skirt. In moments, she was lying with her blouse bunched around her midriff and a pair of pink panties and no more. I was still wrestling with my shirt buttons when Glynnis propped herself up and reached out to undo my belt and then my zipper. I kicked off my shoes and walked out of my pants and except for my socks, we were equal. I leaned over to her and kissed her softly. She pulled me down on top of her and renewed the kiss with tongue and passion. I pulled her panties off and we were off to the races.

I will confess that I pulled my socks off while she was kissing me simply because I have a thing about sex with socks on; it isn't cool. I began to use my tongue, lips and occasionally teeth to work my way south toward the magic delta. I was following a well trod path. Start with the breasts, move to the navel and then to the pussy. Make her happy and horny at the same time and then make sure she gets exactly what she wants. Unless the woman is unusually aroused, she'll know what to expect and if you're any good at all, she'll be a happy partner.

Well, some days, things don't go exactly as planned. Little Glynnis had other ideas. With strength I didn't expect, she pushed me off her before I even got to her navel and jumped on top of me.

"I like to be on top when I get eaten. Then I like to get you ready and then ... well ... you'll find out," she grinned.

"You realize you're upsetting a time tested formula, don't you?"

"It's my pussy and I decide how it gets looked after," she said with a stern look. Then she smiled that lovely smile. "Relax, Lee. I've never been with an older man. I'm really looking forward to this. I'll tell you what I like and you can teach me what you know that I don't."

It all seemed so simple ... except ... I wasn't sure I knew anything she didn't know. In fact, I'm not sure she hadn't already know more than I knew. I guess I was going to find out. I reached over to the nightstand and removed a condom from the drawer. I had taken the precaution of buying some while I was on my walk that afternoon. I knew I wasn't going to make Glynnis pregnant, but she might feel more secure if I used one.

"Do you want me to use this?" I asked.

"Do you need to?"

"Not that I know of. I was just giving you a choice."

"I prefer the real thing. I'm on the pill, so unless you have something I don't want ...?" her voice trailed off.

"Nope ... I'm pretty much a straight arrow. I haven't been with a lot of women." I didn't lie. I just didn't specify a number.

"Fine ... we don't need it. I want the real thing," she said as she began to rub her mons into my abdomen while we talked.

"Okay, little lady. You're in charge of me. Tell me what you want and I'll make sure you get it," I said in a moment of foolish bravery.

"Now you're talking. How 'bout you get my motor runnin' with a little tongue work," she suggested as she began to move up my chest.

There wasn't any point in replying. I grabbed her butt cheeks and pulled her all the way forward and began to dine on her juicy lips and thighs. She was already hot and very wet. I tasted another new flavor and she was delicious. In fact, with my limited know-how, I hadn't had a bad tasting experience yet. She had leaned forward and her hands were now wrapped around the top of the headboard and she was using that to steady herself as I began to work on her pussy.

It didn't take long to discover that she enjoyed oral sex just as much as Constance did. I couldn't see what was happening, but her thighs were clamping along side my head and she was almost dancing on my tongue. The good news was I hadn't even touched her clitoris yet, so there was more to come. She wasn't making any noises that I could hear, but her vaginal contractions told me that I was making my actions count.

I guess I'd been working on her for almost five minutes when I decided to see what happened when I upped the ante. I pushed her ass up a bit so I could get a good look at her pussy, and I could see she had a very small clit and it was tucked back under its hood a bit, despite my efforts so far. I reached around and with my forefinger guessing where the exact location of the little appendage was, I gently stroked the area, moving up in a slow, deliberate motion. I had found Cape Canaveral.

I heard an audible gasp and then she rose as if to escape the touch of my finger. I had no intention of stopping and I was immediately rewarded with her hand moving down to cover mine and pushing it hard against her in a rapid motion. In the meantime, her body was jerking around in a random pattern that made any contact with my mouth strictly a hit or miss proposition. I now had her undivided attention. I brought my other hand around and began to probe her anus.

It was something that Constance had shown me and she said it had really enhanced the erotic sensations when I was eating her. I was now certain that Glynnis was getting the same sensations as well. She still wasn't very vocal, but her breathing and physical response was all the information I needed. I pushed my finger in further and she instantly came. I was welcomed with a face full of her fluids and a mournful, low howl, of what I took to be an approval.

"Oh fuck! That was amazing," she gasped. "Where did you learn that?"

"Oh ... a gentleman never tells," I answered smugly.

"God, if that's what a finger feels like, what would a cock feel like?" she wondered aloud.

"Only one way to find out." I said with a bravado I didn't really feel. I had never had anal sex in my life and I had no idea how to go about initiating it other than what I had read in erotic literature. Lots of lube and go slow. Not much of a how-to manual, I thought.

"Jesus, Lee. Do you think I can try it with you?" she asked tentatively.

"Well, we'll see. There's no rush and I don't want to hurt you. It's not for everyone."

"Yeah ... well ... let's see how it goes ... okay? Maybe later." She didn't sound very sure of herself and that was okay with me. I wasn't anxious to demonstrate my lack of skill and maybe hurt her as well.

We lay beside each other for a few minutes as she came down from her orgasm. We didn't talk. I just stroked her lovely body, paying special attention to those magnificent breasts and her lovely ass.

"Are you a one hit wonder?" she finally asked.

"What does that mean?" I asked, a bit put out by what I thought she might mean.

"I mean, are you good for just one shot and then just roll over and go to sleep?" It was obviously a serious question and I answered it as such.

"No ... especially if the lady would like to continue."

"Good." She was obviously thinking about something. "Most of the guys around here are the 'wham-bam' boys. In quick, off quick, and gone quick." She wasn't saying it with any hint of humor.

"That's too bad. That's very unfair. Many women need time to reach orgasm. Sadly, a lot of guys don't get it."

Glynnis looked at me and then leaned toward me and kissed me gently. "You're not like any of those guys. You're so much more mature and ... caring. I feel really safe with you ... but ... I also feel like I can explore myself with you. You know … try different things and you wouldn't hurt me or … laugh at me."

I smiled at her and kissed her back. "Thank you for your trust. I'm not Superman. I'm just a guy that really loves being with you. I want to make you happy. All you have to do is tell me what makes you happy."

"What makes me happy is you fucking me … now!" she said without a second's hesitation.

I smiled at the crude but honest answer and rolled toward her. I was about to mount her when I changed my mind.

"Want to go for a ride on your new stallion?" I asked, grinning.

"Yes please," she smiled back.

"I'll need you to help get the horse ready."

She reached back to my semi-erect manhood and began to stroke it. She was very good at it and it wasn't long before I was back to full strength.

"You're ready, cowboy," she giggled.

In my best John Wayne voice I said, "Well saddle up, little missy."

She did. I reached for her pussy and it was still very wet and well lubricated. I pulled her up and over my erection while she grasped it, aiming it for her hot tunnel and then began to lower herself. I watched her face. She wasn't a vocal person and you had to listen carefully for the signals and messages she was sending. It was more often in her facial expressions and body language and that meant I had to pay close attention if I wanted to give this lovely young woman the full benefit of the occasion. I paid very close attention.

I let her lead. She started slowly, almost gliding up and down on my shaft with her eyes partly closed and her head turned to one side. She maintained that pace for a few minutes, clearly not in any hurry. For that matter, neither was I. The first change I noticed was her head had started to move around and her eyes were now closed. She was in her own little world and soon that world was going to change. I could feel her vaginal muscles begin to pulse on my cock and she leaned forward, putting her hands on my shoulders.

Her fabulous breasts were now within easy reach and I cradled them in my palms, rubbing her nipples with my thumbs. I was doing whatever I could to enhance the erotic experience for her. It must have had a positive effect as her rhythm increased and her eyes opened, gazing down into mine. I smiled at her and she smiled back at me in a look of total satisfaction. She leaned further forward and kissed me and then pushed herself back up and closed her eyes again. The end was near.

She had once again increased her pace and as she did, I removed my right hand from her breast and again, using my forefinger, I sought her hidden clitoris and began to stroke it in time with her movements. She reacted immediately and her pace became erratic and she had obviously lost her concentration. She was on the edge of her orgasm and I was doing whatever I could think of to help her along.

I began to thrust up into her and that was the final trigger as she opened her mouth and gasped for air as the spasms overtook her body. She continued to ride my cock but she was clearly out of control, overwhelmed by the climax. I gripped her hips to hold her in place and she froze for a moment before going limp and sinking into my arms. During the whole episode, she hadn't said a word or even exclaimed a grunt or groan. It was a completely new happening for me, but I was pleased she had found her destination on this journey.

I had not come. That was unusual and I didn't know exactly why, but I guessed it was because I was so focused on her pleasure that I hadn't really been conscious of my own contribution. I smiled to myself and hugged her to me as her breathing began to return to normal.

"Oh Lee ... that was sooooo good," she said quietly. "I could get addicted to that."

"Just rest and we can play some more later."

"Hmmm ... sounds good," she said lazily, her head on my chest and her hands still on my shoulders.

We stayed that way for quite a while. After a few minutes, I thought she had fallen asleep, but I was wrong.

"You didn't finish ... did you?" she suddenly asked, almost alarmed.

"Just saving up for round two," I kidded.

"How many rounds are there?" she asked as her head popped up and she looked at me with a grin.

"How many would you like?"

"About a thousand like that one."

"Hmmmm … that might challenge me."

"Okay then, how about ….three." she said with an expectant look.

"I think that's within the range of possibility," I answered in a confident voice. "Any special requests?"

"Oh … I like doggie," she said tentatively.

"You don't sound sure."

"Some guys think it's kind of … slutty," she said in a soft voice.

"Some guys are full of it. If it gives you pleasure and doesn't cause you pain or humiliate you … then why would it be slutty?"

She smiled. "I'm glad you think that way. I like it. I really get off on it."

"Do you want to save that for last?"

"Yeah … that would be perfect. But, what do you want to do next?"

"Well let's see … we could do reverse cowgirl," I suggested.

"What's that?"

"Just like the last time except you face the other way."

"What else?" She was paying very close attention now.

"Let me think … Hmmmm … there's the Pile Driver … some call it the Jackhammer. That's when you put your thighs on my shoulders and I rise up and I come down straight into you. It's a great way to finish."

"Wow … there's a lot I have to try," she said sincerely.

I thought for a moment and then tried another tack. "Have you ever done a sixty-nine?"

"No … most guys don't want to … you know."

"No … what do most guys not want to do?"

"You know … eat me. I really love it, but a lot of guys won't do it. They're all hot to get their blow jobs, but not so much for my fun," she said in disgust.

"Well, I think I've already demonstrated I'm not like most guys."

"Yeah … you've done that all right."

"Tell you what … I'm going to show you what the Pile Driver is and then you can revive me when we do a sixty-nine. Okay?"

"You get the best ideas, Lee. I wish you were around here all the time," she said with a smile.

"Don't think I'm not tempted."

I rolled her over on her back and moved down the bed a bit, pushing my arms underneath her thighs and slowly lifting them. She quickly understood to allow her body to bend and her legs to spread in a wide V. I rose above her and aimed my once again rigid cock at her, stroking it over her labia and making sure she was well lubricated. Slowly, I began to press down into her and I heard her grunt as she realized how tight this position made her.

I still hadn't come yet and I was surprised, as well as pleased. It meant that the night was far from over and if Glynnis's curiosity was any indicator, I might extend my new-found repertoire to create even more thrills for the young lady. In the meantime, I was pushing almost vertically into her. My hands were beside her head and I began to increase my pace. I pushed a bit from side to side to see if I could make her breasts move in a rhythmic fashion, but I failed. It was like learning how to use a hula hoop. Some people just never got it and I was one of those.

The good news was that her big boomers were dancing all over the place, just as they had when she was riding me. They had a life of their own and I found it very erotic to watch them. I was certain this time that I would fill her lovely pussy with my semen and I hoped she got something from it as well. I pushed myself up a notch and tried to rub on her clit with my shaft, but I was doubtful it had made contact. Glynnis, for her part, was smiling up at me and clearly enjoying the ride.

When I was younger and just beginning my sexual adventures with women, I had a problem with premature ejaculation. Nothing is more frustrating for a guy than not being able to satisfy his girl because he's finished before she's even started. It took me a long time to work that problem out and gradually I became better. Tonight, however, was one for the books. I felt like I was good to go for an unlimited amount of time. I had never felt this confident before, although my time with Constance certainly helped. I was starting to think I was invincible when that old feeling began in my scrotum and groin.

"I'm coming soon, Glyn," I gasped.

"Go for it, Lee. Drive me hard, big guy." She was smiling and her eyes were big. I wasn't sure, but she might have been approaching an orgasm too.

I put my all into it, or more accurately, into her. I was hammering in and out as fast as I was able and then, with just a couple of seconds warning, I let go.

"Ahhhhh … Glyn … I'm commmming." It was almost painful and I began to relax a bit with the pressure on Glynnis's thighs. I was sweating and drops of perspiration were falling on her belly and thighs. Finally, I backed off and pulled her legs down to the bed. I looked at her and wondered if she had made it too. I was so wrapped up in my own little world, I didn't notice her reaction or expression. My cock slipped slowly out of her and it was followed by a small amount of semen. Oh! Oh! The dreaded wet spot syndrome.

"Oh Lee. You are good. You are very good," she enthused.

"I gather you found that satisfactory?" I enquired in a cheeky voice that hid my uncertainty of just how much she had received from that move.

"It was faaaannnntastic!" I was sure she wasn't trying to fool me, and I was beginning to pat myself on the back for my performance.

We were back to lying on our sides, facing each other and I went back to stroking her lovely body.

"Maybe you are Superman," she said after a bit.

"Naw … just Clark Kent with lessons."

We gazed into each other's eyes and I moved my hand to her face, cupping it tenderly. "Are you okay? I mean, are you feeling okay?"

"Oh … I'm way better than okay. Way, way better," she said with a dreamy smile.

"I have to confess … I was out in space on that last one. I didn't have any idea of where you were … I mean … I didn't know if you had gone with me or not," I admitted.

"Oh yeah. I was with you all the way. All the way." She reached down for my now soft and sticky cock and grasped it, squeezing it slowly. "Looks like we're headed for the big finale," she said.

"There's no rush. We have lots of time. We can save some for tomorrow if you like."

"Oh no you don't. You promised me three and I've only had two plus the lovely tongue job. I can't possibly complain," she announced, "but three is three." She was faking a pout.

"Well then... I guess I have to keep my promise. First, though, I need a rescue. Would you be in favor of that sixty-nine now?"

"Oh yes. Very much in favor."

She was too. She told me earlier she liked to be on top, but the truth was, she just loved being eaten and whether it was up, down, sideways or inside out, she was fine with it. As it turned out, we tried them all. In addition, she had good skills that she plied on my cock. Perhaps not as fabulous as Constance, but very good just the same.

I held off pushing her off the cliff until I was sure she had gotten everything she could possibly have wanted and then I cut her loose. One finger on the clit, a tongue in the tunnel and another finger in her ass and she was done for.

It took her a couple of extra minutes to come down from that one, and I was busy congratulating myself on how clever I was when she turned to me.

"Marry me Lee."

"Huh!" I said, intelligently.

"Marry me. We're perfect together. I would love to have your kids. We could have three or four ... no problem."

It all sounded so simple. So logical. So ... fucking idiotic. It was time to scramble. I had a linebacker and a tackle bearing down on me and I needed to get out of this mess.

"Uh ... Glynnis ... uh ... look ... I'm sorry, but ... uh ... I'm ... uh ... too old for you," I finally blurted.

"No you're not. You're just in your prime and I'm in my best child bearing years," she said seriously.

It was time to bring my fast thinking skills to bear. Too bad I didn't have any. I was really stressed to find an answer that didn't hurt Glynnis but didn't commit me to another marriage and another mistake. Good sex do not necessarily make a good marriage.

"Look ... Glynnis ... I've been married. I know what it's about and I know what makes it work and what doesn't. You have to trust me ... we aren't right for each other. I can't produce children. That hurt my first marriage. You are fresh, young, and vibrant and you have so many opportunities in front of you." I was praying she would understand.

"Lee, I've got one chance in this town. Only one. If I don't make it with him, I'm fucked," she said sadly.

"So, there is a guy? Someone special that you really want?" I asked carefully.

"Yeah. Up 'till now I've been trying out every eligible single guy in town and I don't think he even knows I'm alive. I've got one shot left." It was obvious that she was frustrated and unhappy with her lot in Cranbrook and was looking for a quick fix. I was that fix, in her mind.

"Well, I don't want to hurt your feelings, but I'm not your guy," I said as kindly as I could.

"I know. I know. It's just that ... you treated me so nice, and the sex was so amazing ... well, I thought maybe that you might ...." She never finished the thought.

"I'm sorry, Glynnis. You are a beautiful woman and an incredible bed partner. But ... well ... I'm still working on my rehab. I'm not ready for another commitment. I'm sorry. I'm very sorry."

"Don't be Lee. Besides ... you still owe me a big finish ... remember? Arf! Arf!" she laughed.

I was back to breathing again. She had regained her sense of humor and it was time for that big finish. I had shrunk to a mere shadow of myself and needed to be rejuvenated. Happily, Glynnis saw that too and went to work enthusiastically with her mouth. It didn't take very long for her to bring me back to life and once she had, I used my fingers to create the lubricant she needed. That didn't take very long either. Despite all the activity that evening, we both were ready for more.

She moved in front of me on her hands and knees and I moved behind her, lining my cock up with her well prepared pussy. It didn't take very long to find the opening and begin my assault. I moved slowly and carefully to make sure she wasn't in any discomfort. Within a minute, I had entered her and she was beginning to push back at me and we were on our way.

Like Constance, she was more in the mood for aggressive sex when we did doggie, and she was banging back on me as hard as I was thrusting into her. Again, I was surprised at how I was able to hold back on my finish. If I could figure out what it was that caused this, I would use it every time. As it was, we were pounding away on each other with furious abandon. Soon I could feel Glynnis start to lose her rhythm and erratically grip me with her internal muscles. All that did was make me ready to finish too.

We didn't come together. Glynnis came first and it was a beauty. She twisted and turned and her head flopped all over the place, but still, she didn't cry out. I was happy that she had achieved another climax and with that sense of relief, I came too. It wasn't the mind blower that I had earlier, but it was just great, thank you very much.

As we lay in the afterglow, Glynnis turned to me and kissed me very passionately.

"That may be the best night of sex any woman could possibly have," she said sincerely.

"I'm glad you enjoyed it. I'm just happy I was here to share it with you." I meant what I said. She was a beautiful and dynamic woman. I was almost sorry I wasn't able to commit to her.

"Well, we've still got tomorrow, anyway," she said, looking at me with soulful eyes.

"Are you going to stay tonight? Do I get to wake up with you in the morning?"

"No ... sorry. I have to change and get to work early. I'd love to wake up with you next to me," she said wistfully.

"Dinner tomorrow and then dancing?" I asked tentatively.

"Yup."

"Good ... how about Florio's? I hear the food is great and the family that runs it is very nice."

"Oh ... okay," she grinned. "Meet you there at seven?"

"See you then."

Glynnis was the polar opposite to Constance in every respect except one; she was great in bed. I was once again reminded that this was day six of my sojourn and I had been gifted with five remarkable nights of sex. I had continued on my quest, and I found I was slowly evolving as a different man. I had stopped feeling sorry for myself and was, if anything, gaining a sense of confidence about my relationships with women.

So what if they had virtually dropped themselves into my bed. They don't do that to every guy who comes to town. I had something that made me attractive to them, and I was intrigued with the idea of finding out what it was. In the meantime, there was Glynnis and tomorrow night. I was counting on renewing those two little marks on my ribcage from her fabulous nipples.

Part 3 – Sophia

Glynnis and I had another lovely dinner at her parents' restaurant. This time, she recommended the special, Chicken Marsala, and the choice was, as it had been the night before, perfection. We shared a half litre of Pinot Grigio and continued our conversations from the previous day. I probed gently on who the mystery man might be, but she remained tight-lipped.

She talked a bit about her older brother, Tony, telling me about his success in computer software development in the "big city," Vancouver. They were very close, and I got the impression that Tony was her guardian when she was younger, and that she missed him a great deal since he had moved away.

I had formed the opinion that Glynnis was a very bright and talented young lady, with a lot to offer someone who could handle the special needs she would bring to the bedroom. She was clearly a very sexual woman and would want a man who could complement her desires. But she had a serious, business side, and she would also want that man to match her ambition, her desire to succeed. It was going to take a special guy to be "Mr. Right," and I was wondering if such a man was living in Cranbrook, much less still single.

Shortly before nine, we walked over to the Crowsnest Club and entered. It was just getting going and the noise level wasn't yet at the eardrum bursting stage. The music was largely contemporary pop and I could recognize most of the tunes. A disc jockey was playing the music without comment, but at this time, no one was up dancing and the crowd was pretty thin. I walked to the bar and ordered each of us a drink and returned to our little table.

We sat and talked for a few minutes as we sipped our drinks. I decided that we needed something to occupy our time and I asked Glynnis to dance. We shuffled our way through a few fast numbers and I managed not to embarrass myself too badly. Almost as soon as we took the floor, several other couples joined us, and I was grateful we weren't alone.

After the fast numbers came some slow tunes and I was happy to pull Glynnis to me and hold her closely as we danced together. We might have been a bit of a misfit with our height difference, but I really didn't care. She looked beautiful this evening, wearing a more demure outfit with a pale blue blouse, navy blue skirt and more sensible low heels. Unlike last night, she was wearing both stockings and a bra, and when I stopped to think about it, she was very conservatively dressed.

By ten, I noticed the crowd had grown substantially so as the noise. We were sitting at our table not trying to talk over the music, when I noticed a table with three guys on the other side of the room. Actually, I noticed one of the three guys who caught my attention because he only had eyes for Glynnis. He was nursing a beer and looked more like a college student than one of the locals. I was curious who he might be.

When Glynnis got up to go to the washroom, he watched every step she made until she disappeared down the hallway, his eyes never leaving the entrance until she reappeared five minutes later. Now, I was really interested. There was only one way to find out who he was.

"Glynnis, do you see that table with the three guys drinking beer right across from us?" I asked when there was a break in the music.

"Yeah … why do you ask?"

"You see the dark haired guy in the glasses with the tan shirt … do you know him?" I asked casually.

She looked at him carefully and then back at me with a strange expression. "Sure … that's Peter Barnsley … why do you ask?" she said with a curious look.

"He's been watching you. In fact, he appears to be fixated on you, I think."

"Are you sure?" she asked carefully.

"Yup … damn sure," I said without hesitation.

"Really! Are you absolutely sure?" she challenged me.

"Look … what's the big deal. You're a beautiful woman, and he's interested in you. At least he doesn't look like Elmer Fudd," I cracked.

She looked at me with a strange frown and I thought I could hear the gears turning in her head. She was obviously startled by what I had told her.

"I didn't think he even knew I was alive," she said vaguely as she carefully avoided looking across the room.

"So tell me about him," I requested with a hint of insistence.

"He's a friend of my brother, Tony. He lived in Kimberley, but he went to school here. He used to get a ride into school with his Dad and then back home with him when his dad finished work. He'd go down to his office and do his homework until his Dad closed up. He was Tony's best friend because they were both 'brainiacs.' He's changed a lot. He's been in med school since forever," she finished almost absently.

"So why is it such a surprise he's interested in you?"

"I was just Tony's kid sister. I don't think he even noticed me," she said absently, now looking over to the table of interest.

"Well, I can assure you that has changed. He's definitely noticed you tonight," I said with certainty.

Glynnis turned back toward me and I could clearly see the flushed look on her face and the wide eyed surprise that accompanied it. I smiled. Was this the mysterious guy she coveted as her last chance? I don't think so. This seemed to be a complete surprise to her and it had deeply shocked her when she discovered it.

"Don't you think you should go over there and say hi?" I teased.

"Oh God, I couldn't. I mean … it's been years." She left the thought unfinished.

"Look, Glynnis … you know I'm going to be gone in a day or so, and you're still going to be here. You have to look past the here and now, and think about tomorrow. Maybe there's nothing about Pete Barnsley that will connect with you, but you won't know that unless you try."

I was pretty sure that there was something going on with Glynnis that involved Peter, and I suspected it went back to her school days and her possible infatuation with this guy. I'd seen it before; the little sister grows up and goes from pest to playmate before you even realize it.

She looked at me again with that questioning gaze. She was unsure of herself and possibly a bit frightened. It didn't seem in character for the woman that had virtually attacked me the night before, but there was no denying her uncertainty.

"Go!" I almost shouted as the music pounded in the background.

She got up very tentatively, watching my face and then slowly turned and weaved through the handful of dancers to the other side of the floor. I would have given anything to hear the conversation, but I watched the body language carefully. Peter looked up with a very big smile on his face as she approached, and then stood. When was the last time a guy of his age stood when a woman approached his table? He reached out for her and then hugged her closely to himself. I could almost see the breath and tension drain from Glynnis with that simple gesture and a moment later they were talking a mile a minute to each other, oblivious to the other two guys at the table.

I had to smile. My matchmaking skills had been hidden all these years and then, voila! I leaned back in my chair and let that satisfied feeling wash over me. What the hell, it might have happened anyway, but I was glad I pushed the process. There was only one problem; I had probably just pushed my bed partner off on another guy. At least I didn't feel badly about it. In fact, I felt quite good.

I picked up Glynnis's half full glass of wine and walked carefully across the room to the two reunited friends and placed it on the table in front of them. I don't think they even noticed. I smiled. The two 'spare guys' had moved elsewhere and these two were in a world of their own. I walked over to the bar and ordered another beer.

As I surveyed the room, my eyes fell on a tall, slim, very elegant looking woman of indeterminate age. She was almost as tall as me, I thought. Her long, shining, perfectly straight dark hair fell to the center of her shoulder back, covering an equally elegant looking burgundy blouse. I couldn't see her face except in extreme profile, but I doubted that it would be a disappointment. She had a European look about her, although I don't know exactly why I thought so. She seemed very out of place in this small town dance hall, and I decided to study her before I made any move toward her.

I was watching her and oblivious to what was going on elsewhere when I felt a tap on my shoulder. I jumped at the surprise and turned quickly to find Glynnis looking at me with a flushed face and a giant smile.

"Thanks," was the first thing out of her mouth.

"You're welcome," I replied out of instinct. I sensed her decision to approach Peter Barnsley was being rewarded. "Looks like you two are getting along well."

"Yeah … really well."

"I'm glad. I hope it works out for you, Glynnis. I know that's what you want."

"Yeah." She had become a woman of few words in the space of ten minutes.

I had to laugh. She was hooked and hooked solidly. I leaned forward and kissed her cheek. "Good luck."

She turned and kissed my cheek. "I think he's the one," she whispered.

I looked over at soon-to-be Doctor Peter Barnsley and smiled. I gave him a 'thumbs up' behind Glynnis's back and I saw him visibly relax. It was never a contest.

"Before you go back to your new love," I laughed, "who's the lady in the burgundy blouse over by the bar?"

She turned and looked over and then turned back. "Oh, you mean Sophia Sekich, the 'Ice Queen.' Now that's a challenge," she laughed. "Sorry, Lee, I gotta go." She was looking anxiously at Pete.

"I'll see you tomorrow morning. Have a great time." I was already old news to her.

"Thanks again, Lee. You've really been great. I won't forget you. You're probably the second to the last guy I'll ever make love with," she said with a flounce and a grin.

I watched her head back and rejoin Pete's table, and if she wasn't sitting in his lap, she was damn close. I had a feeling Pete was going to get lucky tonight.

In the meantime, the mysterious Sophia hadn't moved a muscle and continued to sit by herself, watching the dance floor. I guess I had a good dose of self confidence, because I couldn't think of a single reason why she wouldn't want to talk to me. I had gotten used to rejection in my teenage years and I figured, what the hell, I could take as well as I could give. What did I have to lose? I got up and wandered over to her table, approaching her from the side so that I wouldn't startle her.

"Good evening, Sophia," I began. The music was between songs and I didn't have to shout to be heard.

She turned slowly and looked at me like I was some kind of creature from the swamp. "How do you know my name?" she asked in a thick, Slavic-sounding accent.

"I asked Glynnis Florio and she told me."

She looked over to where Glynnis was sitting and then back at me. Her expression had changed from mild contempt to mild interest.

"I do not recognize you. Are you new?" she asked, almost politely.

"Sort of. I'm just visiting while my car is being repaired." I was being careful with what I revealed. I was also interested, very interested. As I looked into her eyes, I was conscious of a woman who was as carefully prepared as a runway model. Her makeup, clothes, bearing, even her attitude seemed to project New York, not Cranbrook. I was on high alert and fascinated. She had an almost Cher-like face; long, thin, and perfect. Her body almost lacked shape from what I was able to see. It was perfect for a model, but lacked the voluptuous curves that wannabe letches like me admired. No big tits, no big ass ... Hmmm.

"Sorry, it's very rude of me to stare, but you are very beautiful," I continued. "My name is Lee ... Lee Stephenson."

She almost smiled and her eyes were appraising me just as I had appraised her. She wasn't about to initiate conversation, so I plowed ahead on my own.

"You don't look like you're from around here. More like New York or Paris, I'd say." I was a blatant attempt to flatter her and surprisingly, it seemed to work. She spoke!

"Montreal. I worked there until I came here to join my parents," she responded in a monotone.

"Were you a model?"

"Yes ... but I got too old," she said simply.

"That doesn't make sense. You don't look ... I mean ... how old is too old?" I stumbled.

She laughed and for the first time, she looked like she might have a personality.

"Some days, twenty one is too old. Some days, maybe thirty. It is a hard business. All work ... no play," she said, losing her smile.

"You said you came here to join your parents."

"Yes … my father was ill. I came to help my mother run their store. He died and now I am here to look after my mother." It was all stated in a matter-of-fact way as if it was exactly what she expected to happen.

"I'm sorry to hear about your father. You must find it difficult to adapt to this town after Montreal."

"Yes and no. I helped my parents when they had a small grocery store in Montreal before I got modeling job. It is not new to me."

"You haven't been here long, have you?"

"No … just a few weeks. My father died just before I got here. I never got to say goodbye," she said sadly. She looked up at me and I began to think that I had almost pierced that tough exterior. It was a protective shell. It stopped her from being hurt, but it didn't always work. The loss of her father obviously hurt far more than the loss of her career. I decided to change the subject.

"May I sit?"

She nodded with the faintest of smiles.

"Your accent … where is your family from?"

"Sarajevo. We left when fighting started. After Olympics, we thought everything would be better but …not so. Old hatreds, old enemies, and friends turn their backs over nothing. It was bad. Papa sold everything and we moved to Canada. It was better. I went to French school, and then the Agency wants me to be a model."

"How old were you?" I asked, fascinated by her story.

"Fifteen. I was tall for girls in my class. I was lucky. They don't treat me badly. I work hard. Soon, I was making a lot of money. Papa look after it for me. I have my picture in catalogues and newspaper and magazines. Then, one day, I am too old. Poof! Not a model any more." She was using her hands to express her sudden career end.

"Do you miss it?"

"No … yes … sometimes." She actually laughed. "I liked being famous. I liked people who see me and then smile like they know me."

"Any boyfriends?"

"Some … not serious. Not any serious one yet," she said, looking directly into my eyes.

"You are very beautiful. I'm surprised you haven't got a flock of guys surrounding you." I meant it sincerely.

"I am spoiled girl. What you call 'high maintenance,'" she admitted.

I laughed. "What does a high maintenance girl do for fun in Cranbrook?"

"She waits for cool guy to come along and ask her to dance," she said smiling at me.

I put a checkmark beside my personal score card and once again patted myself on the back. Perhaps I was invincible.

"Well, I'm not sure how cool I am, but I'd love to dance with you."

She smiled back at me, and when I offered my hand, she took it gently and I led her out onto the dance floor. As luck would have it (and brother did I have it), it was a slow, romantic tune and she slipped into my embrace and we began to move. She was as light as a feather and almost fragile. Her body was slim and willowy, and her scent was intoxicating. I don't think I had ever been this close to someone so exotic. I felt like I was on display. I could feel the eyes of all the guys on me. I had melted the Ice Queen. I had status!

"You are a very good dancer," she said softly in my ear. We were pressed up against each other and I was being very careful to hold her lightly and feel her moves as we slipped across the floor, lost in the music.

"I'm inspired by my partner," I whispered in return. I know! I know! It's corny as hell, but it happened to be the truth. This woman was so completely different and seemingly unreachable, and yet here I was, dancing with her and drawing looks from every guy in the house and quite a few of the girls too. When you're hot, you're hot!

The D.J. took a break for a few minutes and I offered Sophia a drink and she accepted. I got her a glass of white wine and switched to a red for myself. Somehow, beer didn't seem to be the right thing when you are with a woman like this. She excused herself and headed for the Ladies Room, and I sat at my table enjoying the moment. I wasn't alone for long. Glynnis almost ran over to me, sliding to a stop at my table.

"What the hell did you put in her drink?" she asked, wide eyed.

"Nothing, love. Just my natural charm I guess." I was bragging of course, but enjoying my conquest.

"You just got into the Cranbrook Studs Hall of Fame," she declared. "I guess I should have known if anyone could melt her, you could."

"Thanks for the vote of confidence, but I suspect her reputation isn't earned. She just takes a little special handling."

"Well, whatever. You sure made everyone here sit up and take notice. It looks good on her too."

"Thanks. How are things going with Peter?" I asked.

"Super! I've had a crush on him for years, but I didn't think he would even remember me. I was Tony's little pest sister when he was around. I guess he remembered better than I thought," she grinned, almost giggling.

"I take it then that he isn't 'Mr. Last Chance?'"

"No, but I don't think 'Mr. Last Chance' is going to get the chance," she laughed.

"I'm happy for you Glynnis. I hope it all works out for you. I'll be calling you someday to find out."

"Thanks. Oh, here comes Sophia. Good luck," she said as she turned to leave. She didn't make it. Sophia cut her off and reached out for her arm. She leaned in and said a few words into her ear. I wasn't sure what was going to happen until I saw a big smile on Glynnis's face and I decided to relax.

Sophia smiled at Glynnis as the two of them looked over at me, and a moment later, the lithe beauty headed back to our table. I stood up and held out my hand. She took it as I held her chair for her. It seems my manners were improving, as I began to read Sophia better. High maintenance meant she had high expectations of her escorts, and I wanted to show her I understood that.

As she sat down, I was aware that somehow we were closer to each other. I could pick up the delightful scent of her perfume and I had a hard time not staring at her. She was almost impossible to ignore. She commanded my attention and I was happy to provide it. I think she expected that. She wasn't disconcerted by my unconcealed admiration, and in an emboldened moment, I reached for her hand. She allowed me to take it and I held it below the table on my leg. Sophia looked down at her hand and then up at me and smiled, squeezing my hand lightly.

"Dance?" I asked as a slower tune came on.

She nodded and smiled her acceptance, and I held her chair as she rose. She was a woman of few words, but nonetheless, I was having no trouble communicating with her. I began to plot the rest of my evening with this unique lady. I wondered if we would consummate this lovely affair, but to be truthful, it didn't matter as much as I thought it would. I had already achieved a measure of fame and anything more would be icing on the cake. Mind you, I do like icing.

We danced and I talked, she smiled and said a few words, and I reminded myself how much I was enjoying this. My High School skills had been at work and I determined that she was wearing a bra and of course, the lovely burgundy blouse buttoned up the front. Her skirt was black leather, falling well below her knees, the texture and color matching her shoes. Simple observation told me that it had a side zipper. I was fascinated with what her body would look like naked and I tried to imagine, but I was having trouble. Not enough experience, I guess. I was also wondering what she would be like as a lover. Would she be active or passive, loud or quiet, orgasmic or … what?

We continued to dance and then rest, dance some more and then sit and enjoy each other's company, without many words being exchanged. Finally, I took a chance and as she leaned toward me to hear what I might say, I kissed her cheek. She turned toward me and her eyes narrowed. For a moment, I thought I was in trouble, but that thought was erased when she kissed my lips and I felt the slight probe of her tongue. It was time for a decision.

"Your place or mine?" I asked quietly. Now I realize I've used this line before, but let's face it, whatever works, right? And lo and behold, it didn't fail me.

"Mine," she whispered.

I didn't need any more encouragement. I stood, took her hand, and held the back of her chair as she rose. We headed for the coatroom holding hands and with a couple of dollars in the tip jar, we were on our way. I led her to my car and held the door for her, as she slipped into the seat and looked up at me with a smile. She couldn't have done anything more to make me feel as good about this. She gave me directions to her place and we drove off.

Sophia lived in a small duplex on the outside of town, very close to where Straker's B & B was. She unlocked the door and turned on a small table lamp as we entered. She closed the door and, remembering my manners, I helped her with her coat and hung it in the front closet with my own. I turned to her and waited for her to make the first move.

"Would you like something to drink?" she asked with a smile.

"Not unless you would. I'm happy just to be with you," I said quietly.

She smiled and I was struck by how enigmatic it was. It gave away nothing, and I had to remind myself to be patient. I really did not know what to expect.

She walked the two or three steps towards me and her arms circled my neck. She might have been staring me down, but I let that happen as she finally closed her eyes and began to kiss me. It was a soft and yet passionate kiss with her tongue flicking back and forth between my lips. I opened my mouth and she pushed her tongue a bit further into me. I was caressing her body as she concentrated on the kiss. Finally, we parted and she looked at me with a slight smile.

"Glynnis tells me you are a very accomplished lover," she said unexpectedly.

"Glynnis is very generous," I offered quickly after being caught by surprise.

"You did not know we are friends?"

"No, I didn't," I admitted.

"Come with me, Mr. Stey-fan-son," she commanded gently as she led me down the hallway. I kind of liked the European interpretation of my last name. She led me towards one of the two bedrooms. We entered the one on the left as the door on the right was closed. As we passed it, I was almost sure I could see light coming from under the door. I followed her into the softly lit room, admiring her almost effortless stroll. Once a model always a model, I guess.

Her bedroom was very austere, not what I had expected. It had a queen size bed with a simple cherry wood headboard and footboard, and a pair of simple but quality cherry night tables. A matching dresser flanked the inside wall, while a full length mirror was mounted on the closet door. The curtains over a window were drawn closed and they fell almost to the floor. There were no paintings or pictures on the wall and the only pictures on the dresser were of a younger Sophia, and another woman who was obviously her mother. I could instantly see that she was an older version of her beautiful daughter and very lovely in her own right. I turned to Sophia and moved towards her. She turned away from me, but was offering herself for me to undress her from behind.

I reached for the buttons on her blouse, and they almost fell from their eyes. I pulled it gently from her shoulders and revealed her lovely upper body. Her brassiere was a dark red and captured two small teacup sized breasts. I easily removed the bra and was struck by how perfect her breasts were, almost like sculptures, except they were warm flesh and blood, and exquisite in both shape and texture. I palmed them gently for a few moments as I contemplated my next step.

Sophia had closed her eyes and tilted her head back beside mine as I lightly stroked my fingers over her now erect nipples. I took the opportunity to kiss her cheek and nibble on her ear. I was taking this very slowly and I wondered if I wasn't going too slowly for her. I reached for her skirt and after undoing the top button, I lowered the zipper and pushed it down with my hands on each side of her slender hips. She playfully swayed as I pushed the skirt away and then stepped carefully out of it, having already removed her shoes. She wasn't wearing stockings. Her panties were the same dark red as the bra and I left them for now. It was my turn.

I placed my hands on her shoulders and turned her around to face me again. Her eyes had remained closed as I had stroked her breasts, but they were open now and she was looking searchingly into my eyes. I smiled at her, hopefully giving her confidence that we would soon enjoy our union, but first, there was the matter of my clothes. I began to pull my shirt out of my pants and she reached for my buttons to help me. I unbuckled my belt and began to undo my pant's zipper and step out of them while she finished with my shirt. In less than a minute, we were facing each other wearing only our underwear and she led me to the bed and sat on the edge facing me.

I lay on the bed and pulled Sophia down in my arms. I began to kiss and fondle and nibble and pinch and generally make love to this slender beauty. Her hand had gone to my cock and had softly gripped it and began stroking me to erection. Amazingly, I had not been in a state of arousal and it was another phenomenon that I hadn't experienced before. It didn't bother me since she had quickly corrected that condition, but nonetheless, it was another new thing to ponder in my new world. I pushed the thought out of my mind and got on with my responsibilities.

I slipped to the floor on my knees and began to remove her panties. I was in for another surprise. For the first time I encountered a completely hairless pussy. I had never seen one before up close and it was both exotic and erotic. It suited this woman perfectly. I should have expected it I suppose, but it I didn't. I gazed at it and then looked up at Sophia's face. She was watching me expectantly. I smiled and bent to my task. I started to stroke the entire length of her pink slit with the top of my tongue, traveling as far down as the perineum and slowing drawing it up to just short of where her clit would be. I spent more than a couple of minutes preparing her for my next touch.

I brought my arms around her lovely, slim thighs and my fingertips stroked her hairless mons. She was moving slightly under my tongue and I lifted my head and my fingers moved to her sex and gently parted her lips. Like everything else about her, it revealed more perfection. I could also see that her clit was prominent and I was ready to move to that target when I resumed my worship of her magnificent body. She may not have been my ideal woman in shape, but she was like a fine piece of jewelry; you had to admire the beauty of design.

I resumed my tongue work and this time I allowed it to travel all the way to the clitoris and I got the immediate response I was hoping for. Her body arched and I heard a gasp as she reacted to the touch on her sensitive nub. I went back to it again and again and each time I was rewarded with her reaction. I looked up briefly and saw that her eyes were closed and her body rigid in expectation, her hands tightly gripping the sheets by her side. I decided to take her all the way if I could, and I stayed with a steady stroke on her labia and clit. It didn't take her very long to reach her release and I heard as well as felt it expressed by her whimpering cry and her rigid torso. I moved her to the bed, guiding her to lie on it.

I crawled up on the bed and lay beside Sophia as she came down from her orgasm. She had turned her head toward me and her eyes were blinking as she stared at me. I touched her cheek with my fingertips and she smiled and reached for me. She was obviously pleased with my beginning and soon she was fondling my semi-erect cock and bringing it up to full potential. There was no doubt she knows what was expected next.

I rolled over on top of her, carefully spreading her legs as I prepared to enter her. We were both very ready and I aimed my rigid cock at the now obvious entrance and pushed slowly but steadily forward for a couple of inches. She seemed tight, but was reaching for my hips to pull me in. I took that as an invitation and I continued to push steadily until I was finally touching bottom. Sophia was tense, but it seemed to be with expectation rather than concern.

I began to move, very slightly and slowly at first, but gaining a bit of distance on my stroke as I watched her carefully. Her reaction was positive. She was smiling slightly and her hips were moving with me. We were on our way. It wasn't that long before we were really humming. I had that invincible feeling back again and I wasn't worried about it coming to a premature end. I just let it all hang out and we were really rockin' and rollin'.

Like Glynnis, Sophia wasn't verbally expressive but I didn't have any doubt that she was with me all the way and she was enjoying herself. I just kept plowing into her and she just kept pushing back at me as we headed for a big finish. I could feel the beginning of the end and I hoped that Sophia would be right there with me.

"I'm getting close … Sophia," I gasped.

She reached up with her hands and grasped my head, covering my ears. Her eyes were wide and she was breathing as heavily as I was. The end was pretty close for both of us and I realized she was going to finish first as she clamped onto my head by the ears, shut her eyes and arched her back, all the while holding her breath. Suddenly, she let go, her breath whooshing out of her and her body slamming back onto the bed. I wasn't far behind, and within a few seconds I let go and splashed my semen into her in four strong pulses.

I lay beside her, face down in the pillow for a couple of minutes while I regained my breath. It had been an almost frantic session that I hadn't expected from this otherwise quiet woman. What is it they say about the quiet ones. "Ice Queen" my ass! She had just worn me out. Both of us looked whipped and when she turned out the light, I snuggled up against her, holding her close to me. She was obviously inviting me to stay for the night and I wouldn't think of turning her down.

One side of my ass was parked over the wet spot but it didn't really bother me. Once again I praised whatever god was looking after me. It was another spectacular night with another spectacular woman. I was almost afraid to pinch myself to see if it was real. It wasn't very long before I had drifted off to sleep, probably only seconds after Sophia.

Sometime in the middle of the night, I awoke to the strangest feeling. It was pitch black and I couldn't see my hand in front of my face, but something felt very different. It took me a moment or two to get my brain in gear and assess what was happening and then, when I did, I still couldn't figure out what the hell was going on. I had my arm over Sophia, cupping a breast with one hand and the back of my other hand was snug against her ass. So far so good.

The confusing part was the feel of a pair of breasts sticking into my back, the feel of another female body curled around my backside and a warm, soft hand stroking my cock. That's just too many body parts I figured, even in my partly conscious state. It finally came to me that we had a new partner in bed and I was about to say something when Sophia rolled toward me and kissed me.

"I will come back later. Enjoy yourself and treat Momma like you treat me," she whispered.

Holy shit! Her mother had climbed into bed with us and was all set for me to screw her, and on top of that, it was okay with her daughter. What kind of a fucked up family was this? In the meantime, Momma was working my cock over pretty good and I was getting hard again and after all, I really should be a gentleman and accept the hospitality of the hostess. So ... aw, what the hell!

I rolled over toward my new partner and began to explore her body in the dark. I had only just got started when I realized I had forgotten my manners.

"Hello ... my name is Lee," I said quietly.

"Anna ... nice to meet you," she said and I could almost detect a smile in her voice.

I had to laugh. This was truly bizarre. First I screw the daughter, then Momma wants in on the action. Oh well … if I have to, I have to. I slipped my hand down to her thighs and she willingly parted them. Unlike her daughter, Anna had what felt like a normal complement of hair on her pussy. I couldn't have cared less. I pulled her to me and kissed her, pushing my tongue between her lips and she willingly opened her mouth to accept me. I was stroking her sex with my fingers as we kissed and not knowing what she was expecting, I thought I would use the time honored order of things, working my way south before I explored the tunnel of love.

It seemed to meet with Anna's approval, but then, when I thought about it, I wondered if she had enjoyed any sex since the illness and death of her husband. The more I thought about it, the more I wanted to make this special for her. I was wide awake now. I had never met the woman, but my memory conjured up an image based on the photograph on Sophia's dresser. My exploration of her body had told me two things; her breasts were considerably larger than her daughter's, and her hips were wider, leading to a more fulsome backside. It was a nice change and another new experience.

There was another difference between the two women. Anna was vocal. Very vocal! As I sucked and licked and nipped and pinched her nipples, she told me very clearly she was enjoying the attention I was paying to them. So … I paid extra attention to them before I started down toward her navel. She wasn't expecting that and she jumped when I stuck my tongue in her belly button cavity and swirled it around. She squealed her delight and squirmed under my ticklish torture, but she made no attempt to put a stop to it.

I was pretty sure Sophia could hear us, or at least her mother. I smiled at the thought and wondered what other sounds I could extract from this expressive mature woman. As I reached her pussy, I could smell her arousal and I was anxious to savor yet another new taste in this smorgasbord of females I had encountered in the last week. Each had been unique and each had been delightful in their own way. Anna was no exception.

I did what I always do; I started slowly and ignored the clitoris until I had established my partner's arousal. Anna continued to verbally respond, and I think, encourage me. I think so, but she was speaking her native language and I couldn't understand a word, although I could clearly understand the exclamation points. I heard "Ya" a lot, so I assumed I was doing okay.

Finally, I thought I would move the process along and I pushed a finger into her pussy and began to stroke her. Again, her response was immediate and approving. I added a second finger and went searching the roof of her vagina for the G spot. I must have found it because she told me so … I think. Anyway, she was dancing on the end of my fingers, and I was happy with her unmistakable sounds of pleasure.

I was enjoying myself, and the only thing that would have been better would be a bit of light so that I could see my lover's face and read the reactions and emotions she was experiencing. Oh well, you can't have everything. It left a bit of mystery about Anna, something yet to discover. I withdrew my fingers and tasted the nectar of this wonderfully mature goddess. It was time to enter her and complete this union.

I moved up over her and she immediately grasped my erection to guide me properly in the darkness. I entered her and slipped effortlessly in all the way to my groin. She was very well lubricated and I wasted no time in beginning my stroke. She became quite animated almost immediately, and I could only assume she hadn't had a man inside her for quite some time. She was almost desperate in her actions and she clamped onto my ass with both hands, urging me farther into her than I could possibly go. I needed to find a better solution for her and in a moment of inspiration, I pulled out of her.

I heard her gasp of shock when I left her, but quickly showed her I wanted her to turn over and she immediately turned, and anticipating my intention, stuck her lovely ass up in the air and was on her knees awaiting my entry. I moved forward until I found her saturated pussy with my hand and then carefully guided my cock into her. I knew she would be getting more of me and in addition, I would be able to massage her clit as I stroked into her. It was the perfect storm for Anna and she exploded into action as I drove strongly into her and my fingertip touched and then massaged her clit. She went wild.

I'm sure the neighbors must have heard her howl, not to mention her daughter. I have to admit, I love making love to a woman who holds nothing back and tells you exactly how she feels about your performance. I didn't have to speak her native tongue to know I had hit the jackpot. I just flat out fucked her silly. I didn't need to last very long, but since I had already unloaded into her daughter, I was going to last for a little while anyway.

It ended the way you would expect. She had one big, volcanic orgasm and she announced it to all the world before collapsing on the bed in what I assumed was exhaustion. I didn't finish, but I didn't really care. I was more interested in satisfying this sex starved woman and hoping it was what she wanted. I lay beside her and pulled her to me, kissing her and stroking her as she came down from her trip. I didn't want her to feel any different than any other lover I would have. She may have been a surprise, but I still felt I owed her my best effort.

I think I made a new friend. Well, for that matter, two new friends. As the chaos subsided and the noise level dropped, I saw the bedroom door open and the light from the other bedroom illuminated the wreckage of our bed. Sophia crept into the room and sat beside me, her hand stroking my head.

"I think you have made Momma very happy," she whispered.

I reached up and pulled her down for a kiss. "You are full of surprises," I said softly.

She laughed quietly and lay down beside me. Her mother turned to her and said something in her first language and Sophia responded in a calm voice. Her mother laughed and rose from the bed.

"Momma says this bed is a mess and we should all move to her bed."

"Tell your Momma thank you and if it's okay with you, it's okay with me."

We padded over to the adjacent bedroom and for the first time, I could see Momma in all her glory. She was nearly sixty I guessed, but had the body of a forty year old in most respects. Her breasts sagged a bit and her tummy was slightly rounded, but not so much to discourage me. Her hair was gray, but it was an elegant, swept back coiffure and with her height and wonderful posture, she was a striking woman and it made me wish once more that I had been able to make love to her with some light to watch her.

Momma said something to her daughter and Sophia laughed and turned to me.

"Momma says you get the middle. She wants to taste you," she said laughing.

"Oh, does she now. Just what does she want to taste?"

"You will find out," she said with a wink.

Why did I get the feeling that I might not be getting much sleep that night? I glanced at the clock and was surprised to see that it was just after one o'clock. Well, I guess it wasn't that late, and I had gotten a nap before meeting Glynnis. All in all, not that bad, I smiled to myself.

I was getting a bit arrogant with this new power over women that I had somewhere acquired. At least I was conscious of it and I would do everything possible not to reveal my feelings to these women. This was just too good to screw up.

I climbed onto the bed and centered myself in the middle, waiting for my two lovely bedmates to join me. Sophia was first and Anna followed her after turning out the light. She had drawn open her curtains slightly and as my eyes adjusted to the dark I could make out our shapes in the limited light from outside. Sophia had turned toward me and was kissing me and holding my hand. I was lying on my back when Anna pushed herself up and moved down my body until she was staring right at my manhood. She grasped my soft member in her warm hand and lowered her mouth to it.

Anna started off slowly, kissing the glans and using the tip of her tongue to tickle me to life. Naturally it worked, and soon I was erect and ready again. At that point, Anna took me in her mouth and began to seriously use her tongue and lips and generally make love to my cock. She must have been enjoying herself because she was humming as she sucked on me and the vibration was making me crazy. I'd never experienced it before and I was quickly heading for an eruptive ending.

"Anna ... I'm getting close," I warned.

She looked up and smiled at me and went right back to her work. Sophia didn't say a word and I could only assume it was her intention to let her mother do whatever she wanted.

I didn't last much longer. I'd heard about a "hummer," but I had never been exposed to one before. It was wild and while I was able to stall my finish during regular sex, I had no hope of slowing this new event down at all. I just gave in and let it happen. I tried once again to warn Anna, but she just kept on keepin' on.

She took everything I had and never even looked up. It was hard to reconcile her actions over the past hour with her age. She was a very active woman, and it occurred to me that she badly needed a man in her life. The loss of her husband had not subdued her libido, and she would be a handful for any two guys. In the meantime, I was flat on my back again and having a hard time wiping the smile off my face.

It was Sophia's turn next and I wondered if I could get it up one more time. I had my doubts, but I was willing to try if she was. In the meantime, Anna had slipped up beside me again and we were kissing very passionately as I thanked her for another wonderful encounter. Sophia had slipped down and was considering my now limp member. She hadn't touched it yet and since I was occupied with Anna, I didn't really notice what she was doing. I found out in a hurry.

At first it was her fingertip almost imperceptibly touching the base of my scrotum and gliding toward my anus. Now, if you want a stimulating experience, let your lover do that to you a few times. I'm sure Anna could feel the reaction I was having to her daughter's little game. But Sophia was only getting started. She put her mouth on my cock and still persisted with that finger thing that was really getting my attention. Now I was distracted. I was supposed to be thanking Anna but her daughter was getting most of my attention.

I looked down at Sophia, and Anna did as well. She must have known what her daughter was up to because she smiled and just lay back and watched. In the meantime, Sophia was beginning to get results, but what she did next, changed everything. Her delicate little finger didn't stop at the edge of my anus. This time she pushed it in and I must have jumped a foot. The last time I had a finger in my ass was last year's prostate exam, and it wasn't anywhere near as wild as this. My cock almost jumped to attention, and I was left open mouthed, completely focused on what she was doing to me. Her finger was stroking my prostate and within no time at all, I was hard as a rock.

At that point, Sophia knew exactly what to do. She mounted me, guided my manhood into her hot, slick center and we were joined once again. She danced on top of me with abandon; up and down, side to side and round and round. She was having fun and it was contagious. I must have had a smile as big as a clown because that's the way I was feeling. Once again, I was reminded that sex could be fun too.

I don't know when we all finally fell asleep, but I didn't really care. It was an uninhibited frolic, and an adventure I had never expected. In the back of my mind, I wondered if this was a 'one off' or was there more to it. It seemed completely spontaneous, and yet there didn't seem to be any hesitation or confusion when Anna entered the scene. As I drifted off to sleep, I thought I would ask some questions in the morning.

When I awoke the next morning, I discovered that I was alone in the bed. I could hear the shower running in the bathroom, and I could smell breakfast cooking in the kitchen. I rolled out of the bed and in my naked state, wandered over to the other bedroom to collect my clothes. I dressed and strolled down to the kitchen. As I entered, Anna turned and smiled at me.

"Breakfast is almost ready," she said in almost perfect but accented English.

I stopped dead for a moment and then smiled at her. "You've been playing games with me," I said with a grin.

"It made things more interesting, don't you think?" she winked.

I laughed. "Oh yeah … very interesting." I walked to her and embraced her, kissing her and smiling all the while. I think sometime last night I had figured it all out.

I sat at the kitchen table, admiring the mature beauty before me when Sophia entered, wearing a robe and looking very fresh.

"Good morning, Lee," she said, bending to give me a kiss.

"Good morning to you too."

I was hungry and I wanted to eat, but I also wanted to test my theory out on just what had happened last night. Once again, it was time to be patient. Anna soon placed a full plate of what I could only describe as an oversized breakfast in front of me. Eggs, potatoes, bacon, tomatoes, toast and coffee. It was enormous and far more that I was used to for a breakfast.

"You know what they say, Lee. Breakfast is the most important meal of the day," Anna said seriously.

"Important yes … biggest … not usually," I laughed.

Soon we were all eating and there was little conversation. I admit … I ate most of it. I laid off the potatoes, but the rest of it was gone in a heartbeat. I really was hungry. These two women nearly wore me out last night.

"All right ladies. Time for confession," I said out of the blue.

They looked up at me in surprise, Anna with an especially cautious gaze.

"What do you mean?" Sophia asked.

"I mean, just how did I end up in bed with two beautiful women?" I asked with a non-nonsense tone.

They looked at each other and then at me and then back at each other and then Sophia burst out laughing. The jig was up.

"You think you know?" Anna asked.

"Well ladies, I think Sophia invited me back here for her own purposes, and you and she have an agreement that you share the men she brings back. Am I right?"

"Very good, Mr. Steyfanson," Anna said. "How did you discover our … secret?"

"Well, two things actually. First, I saw Sophia and Glynnis talking and I know they were comparing notes on me. Second, Sophia wasn't surprised when you came into her room and joined us in the bed. She just left like it was an everyday thing. I think Sophia has been keeping you supplied in lovers."

"Are you offended?" Anna asked.

"Not in the slightest. I enjoyed every moment of it," I answered honestly.

"Good. I enjoyed it too. You are very accomplished lover," Anna offered.

"Thank you for the compliment. But then, both of you are very beautiful women, and a man would be a fool not to be inspired by being with you."

"You are very generous, Lee. My Bronco was a powerful lover. I miss him so. I have needs and Sophia helps me. You are not angry that we did this?"

"No … not at all. I understand how difficult it must be for you. I hope you find someone who can be what you need."

"At my age, I am not hopeful. But if Sophia can bring me wonderful young men like you, I will be okay," she laughed.

I looked at Sophia and she was smiling and enjoying the conversation. There was no embarrassment at my discovery of their plot, and they correctly assumed that after I left, life would go on as before. I had to admire their audacity. It was as bold as it was devious, but it seemed to work. At least it did on me.

We finished the breakfast and I helped them clean up the dishes and finally had a shower. I felt a bit better, but I needed a shave sooner or later, so I decided to head back to Straker's to clean up before I went to Glynnis's tire shop and get my car back to full operational status. I hugged and kissed both these wonderful ladies and we promised to keep in touch. I was particularly interested in hearing from Anna. I wanted her to find someone to replace her beloved Bronco. She deserved at least that, and Sophia would do anything for her as well. Family counts for a lot, I thought.

I said my final good-byes and headed back to Straker's to collect my stuff. After I shaved, brushed my teeth, paid my bill, and thanked them for their hospitality, I headed for the tire store. I pulled up in front and walked in to find Glynnis in her usual place behind the counter, and looking after another customer. Her uncle walked into the office, spotted me, and smiled.

"I've got that tire. If you give me your keys, I'll get in on right away and you can be on your way," he said cheerily.

I had half a mind to ask him if he was trying to get rid of me, but thought better of it. He was a nice guy and he had done everything I could have asked of him. I passed him the keys and turned my attention back to Glynnis. Her customer headed for the waiting area and I approached the desk.

"Hi … good morning," I said with what I hoped was a cheery voice.

"Hi Lee. Good to see you. How did you make out last night?" she asked with a sly look.

"Fine thanks. Of course, you knew what I was in for … didn't you?"

She laughed. "I hope you enjoyed it."

"Oh yes. I did that all right. But more importantly, how did you and Peter make out."

"We … made out," she said cautiously.

"So, is he still in the hunt for 'Mr. Right?'"

"No. He's way past that," she laughed.

"Good … I'm glad. Should I ask you how he made out last night?"

"No … but then, since you had such an important part in it, I can tell you that he's inexperienced, but willing. I think I can teach him. He has more than one important quality, but the main one is that he is a 'big man,'" she giggled.

I almost said something silly and then caught her meaning. "Oh … well then … that's all good isn't it?"

"Yeah … it's all good."

I settled my bill, leaned over the counter and kissed her cheek, smiled and walked out to my car. Uncle Jack handed me the keys and I slid into the driver's seat, took a final look at the office, waved, and headed off.

I drove north on Highway 95 for an hour before my mind caught up with me. I spotted a gas station with a convenience store attached and pulled in. I was not thinking properly. I was in turmoil without the trauma. My life had changed so dramatically that I had no idea how to cope. I had been with four women in a matter of six days and I had developed a belief that it was inevitable. Women just naturally gravitated to me. It was little more than a juvenile wet dream and yet, it was real.

I needed some time to work this out. I had been married to Jocelyn for ten years. Ten years of vanilla sex and declining emotions. In the space of six days, I had gone through some sort of catharsis, and I wasn't the Leighton Philip Stephenson that I knew. I was happy with my newfound sexual prowess, but concerned that I didn't understand it. I needed some time to myself to figure out what was going on with me. I might not have a destination in mind, but I was on the move again.

Part 4 – Beth:

I sat in my car in the parking lot of a convenience store for quite a while. I had long finished the wretched coffee that they offered, but I was lost in my thoughts. A wise man once said "never look a gift horse in the mouth," but that's exactly what I was doing. I had left my old surroundings less than a week ago, and it was as if I had stepped through some portal into a parallel universe.

I was living in a fantasy land of willing women and unlimited sex. I kept wondering when all will come to a crashing halt, and I would be returned to my mundane existence. The magic that had enhanced my short, new life seemed to continue without any assistance from me. I began to think perhaps I didn't really need to do anything but hang on for the "ride."

When little kids misbehave, parents often give them what they refer to as a "time-out," a little private time alone to think about their behavior. I was pretty sure I needed a time-out. I certainly needed to think about my behavior. I also needed to try and figure out just who Leighton Philip Stephenson had become. I was certainly not the man who married Jocelyn Campbell ten years earlier. I may have been the guy who had the responsible and generally interesting job as an insurance investigator. I wasn't a virgin when I married Jocelyn, but I certainly didn't have the skills and know-how that I had picked up in the past six days.

When our marriage petered out and was put to a merciful end, I made the biggest decision of my life. I quit my job, cashed in my chips, took a sabbatical from my old life, and went looking for a new one. In my back pocket I had a job offer from Orca Investigations that would be at least as interesting as my old job and probably even more. My friend, Pete Dennison, had been pestering me to join them, but because he understood my need to escape for a while, his boss was holding the offer open indefinitely. You can't lose when you have friends like Pete.

But back to my problem. Now I realize not every guy would think of the last six days of my life as a problem. In fact, they would probably think I was paranoid, or at least mildly psychotic, for complaining about what had occurred. But the truth is, my life during these past six days bore no resemblance to my life for the previous thirty-four years.

I had lived a pretty ordinary, low-key existence, and I behaved as any normal working husband would. I got up, shit, shaved, showered, had breakfast, brushed my teeth, drove to work, came home had dinner, watched some TV or read a book and went to bed. Once or twice a week, I would make love to my wife, and other than the weekends, that was pretty much my every day life.

When I broke that bond with my routine, everything changed. Maybe they have'nt all happened this week, but the really weird stuff had. My encounters with Constance, Glynnis, Sophia, and Anna were sequential and almost, it seemed, inevitable. It was as if they had been preordained. Now, I know it sounds goofy, but that's how it appeared to me.

So to save my sanity and try to find an answer to this conundrum, I am going to abstain from interaction with females for at least few days. I hadn't decided on how many, but I thought it would be more than two. I also decided I would start to keep a diary of my travels and adventures. It would be a way of recounting this strange voyage, while giving me something to keep me occupied at the same time. Decision made, I headed for my next destination point, Fairmont Hot Springs.

The Mountain Meadows B & B was an Alpine style home with three guest suites in the loft, each with an ensuite. When I phoned that morning, there was one room available and I immediately booked it. I was a bit surprised at how busy they were, but I remembered that the area was known for corporate retreats. Nestled right in the heart of the Rockies, the skiing would last considerably longer than near the coast.

I arrived in mid-afternoon and checked in with the hostess, Sandra Melling. As usual, this was a family business, and while they preferred I don't check in until four o'clock, I was given a break since the room was ready and they were almost finished with their chores. I dropped my bag and laptop in my room, surveyed the facilities, grabbed my digital camera, and left to explore the area.

It was a fairly cloudy day and the mountains were somewhat obscured with a low overcast, but it was easy to see the attraction of the area. The Rockies are majestic at any time, and the magnitude of the rock faces and upheavals from so many millions of years ago is always spectacular. I felt pretty insignificant in these surroundings.

I drove around the little town and found a couple of likely restaurants. I had booked my room for three nights in anticipation of my hiatus from hedonism. The town was pretty small, and I hoped I could find enough things to fill my time. Just before five, I headed back to the B & B to start my diary and record some thoughts. It didn't take long to get going, and when I next looked up at the clock on the wall it was almost seven. I took a break and headed off towards the town. I ate by myself, pen and notebook by my side to record any thoughts or remembrances of these past few weeks, and more importantly, the last six days.

I was oblivious to my surroundings in the restaurant. I was seated by a young lady of nondescript features and my waitress was equally forgettable. Good! I wasn't distracted, and neither they nor I were likely to fall under whatever spell had been cast. I finished my meal and as I was savoring the remains of a nice Chilean red, I looked around at the other patrons. Besides the nearby young woman, there were two older couples at different tables, another table of four younger people, and that was it. There was nothing to command my attention. I finished the wine and signaled the waitress for the check and prepared to leave. Then, as I looked up, an absolutely stunning young woman walked in, looked around, saw me, nodded, and smiled.

As Jack Nicholson so aptly put it, "I was just inches from a clean getaway." I sat frozen in place. I felt powerless to move; certainly to leave. She was a dazzling redhead of about thirty years and she was tall. Her hair was long and very curly, her face was that perfect oval shape every woman wishes for, and there was a lovely sprinkling of freckles across the bridge of her long, aquiline nose and the tops of her cheeks. She was lean, yet still very voluptuous. A nice hip flare that was accented by a tight, long, grey wool skirt, while her more-than-adequate breasts were snugly confined in a dark forest-green sweater. A wide black belt and black low heels were the only accents on this beauty and they were more than enough. On top of all that, she looked vaguely familiar.

She was by herself sitting in a table that was directly in front of me, giving me a complete view of her in profile. It was now a battle of wills. Could I simply pay the bill and leave, or would I be tempted to introduce myself and see what effect my new powers would have on her. Incredibly, my waitress chose that very moment to bring my bill and stand directly in front of me, blocking my view of the mystery woman. Damn! Well, it was the excuse I needed. I pulled out some bills, left a reasonable tip and walked to the exit. I turned briefly to look back at her one more time, sighed, and left. I had managed a small but important victory ... but only just.

I returned to my room in the loft and opened my laptop. I reread my musings from the afternoon and thought for a moment about where to continue. There was so much to say, and the only path to take was to record it all and edit from there. I set to it and by ten I had fifteen pages of notes, comments, remembrances, and observations. Mountain Meadows was equipped with wireless and I surfed around for a few minutes, gathering the news and checking my e-mail. I signed off for the night and went to bed. I was asleep in seconds.

I awoke with the realization that it was a Saturday morning and my one week anniversary was upon me. I had finally put one night behind me that had been free of sexual involvement with a woman. One down, two to go. Go ahead, laugh! Everyone has to have a goal in life. Mine was to avoid having sex for three nights in a row. Doesn't sound like much, does it? Well, we'll see.

I joined the other three guests for breakfast, and as usual lately, I ate more than I was accustomed to. The food was great and irresistible, so I didn't resist. I went back to my room and resumed my diary where I had left off the night before. I banged out my thoughts on the almost silent keyboard for an hour or so and then hit save, picked up my jacket and headed out to the car.

I slipped into the seat, started the engine and then just sat there. I had no idea where to go, so I pulled out my topographical map of B.C. and had a look at where I was and what was nearby. I found a back road up a valley to what appeared to be an open area, and since the weather was good I decided to try my luck up there and do a bit of hiking. After all, I needed the exercise. I'd had enough breakfast to last me until supper time, so there was no need for anything but water and I could pick that up along the way.

When I got to the end of the narrow, rough road, I was surprised to see a mid-size SUV sitting off in an open area of grass, so I parked my Outback nearby. I grabbed a couple of water bottles and started to walk up the incline of the meadow. There was no one in sight, but since it was a big meadow, that wasn't surprising. I walked for a half hour or so, stopping now and then to take some pictures of the marvelous scenery.

It wasn't a few minutes later when I came over a rise and spotted a figure ahead of me. At first, I couldn't tell if it was coming or going, but soon I realized it wasn't moving at all. As I get closer, there was something familiar about this person, and a couple of minutes later I was sure of what it was. I was also sure of whom it was. The tall redhead was standing in a field of alpine flowers and looked to be making notes on a pad. I was pretty sure it was the woman from the restaurant, and as I get closer, my suspicion was confirmed. I realized she wasn't making notes, but sketching with a pencil. I made enough noise so that I don't startle her and continue to approach.

She looked up in surprise as I come towards her from the side. That same big smile broke out on her face as she apparently recognized me as well.

"Hi," I said with a smile.

"Hi … you're a long way from home," she said casually.

I wasn't sure what exactly she exactly meant. My old home was certainly a long way away. Other than last night, I didn't have any sense that I had met her before. I was confused.

"I'm sorry … have we met before?"

"I'm not surprised you don't remember, Lee." She held out her hand and I took it. "I'm Beth Jorgenson. I'm Brian Tennyson's P.A."

"Oh, Beth … of course. I apologize for not recognizing you." Brian Tennyson was my former employer's executive vice president. I seldom saw him in the course of my work, and would have only seen Beth Jorgenson in passing.

"No apology necessary," she smiled as she casually examined me. "You're a bit of a celebrity around the office."

"How so?"

"You quit a great job just before they were about to promote you to department head. You just told them you needed some time and space and that you likely wouldn't be back," she said with a rueful smile. "Not many guys have the guts to do that."

"Well ... there were special circumstances," I suggested.

"You mean your wife?" she asked with a raised eyebrow.

"Ex-wife."

"I'm sorry, that was thoughtless and inconsiderate of me," she said.

"Not a problem. It was a bloodless parting."

"And then you vanished."

"Well, I don't know about vanished. You found me," I chuckled.

"True. When I saw you at the restaurant last night, I was surprised. I thought you might have headed for some glamour spot like Las Vegas or the Riviera."

"Why would you think of that?" I was curious about what she was thinking.

"A handsome, available young man with great prospects, looking to forget? Maybe it's what I would do in the same circumstances."

"Uhhhmmm." It was as non-committal as I could be. I was beginning to sense that strange feeling again. Where was this encounter heading? She was such a commanding presence. She is very tall, at least as tall as me, but she is undoubtedly very feminine. Was she coming on to me? Was it starting all over again?

"Cat got your tongue?"

"Yeah ... I guess."

"Well ... I'm used to it. I usually intimidate the men I meet."

"It's not intimidation," I said bluntly, and perhaps with a bit more force than I had intended.

"Oh ... so ... what is it then?" She challenged me without hesitation.

"Long story ... no ... that's not right. Short story ... six days long."

"Good. Short stories are easy to remember." She was grinning during this banter.

"Sorry ... not for public consumption." I turned away, looking to change the topic. "You were sketching. Is it your hobby?" I asked, turning back to her.

"Yes. I sketch, and then I paint."

"Here, or at a studio?"

"Here ... if the weather allows. Otherwise, I take a picture and use that to help my memory."

"You've walked a long way for a painting."

"I didn't realize how far. I just kept moving until I thought I was in the right place to get the image I wanted. I guess I was dazzled by the scenery and forgot where I was."

"Well ... I'm here to help. What can I get you?"

"Nothing ... except ... Uhhhmmm ... I could use a drink of water," she said, eyeing my two bottles.

"Of course. Please help yourself." I passed one of the bottles to her. When her hand touched mine, I felt that tingling feeling again. Shit! Here we go again!

"Why are you so ... wary of me?" she asked out of the blue.

"Same short story ... same reason for no answer."

"Bullshit!" she spat without venom. She had my undivided attention.

"What's the matter, never heard a woman swear before?"

"Nope ... I mean yes ... I've heard women swear before. I'm just wondering what the big deal is."

"I think I intimidate you. You think I'm too big or too pushy or too ... something," she said, not looking at me as she resumed sketching.

I laughed out loud. "Lady, I'm an investigator. I see the seedy side of life way more often than you would realize. I am definitely not intimidated."

"Not the same," she said simply, continuing with her sketch. "Some men are overwhelmed by some women. It's an ego and comfort thing. Trust me ... this I know."

"Well ... for the record ... you don't frighten me or intimidate me," I stated flatly. "You can take that to the bank."

"OK ... so let's say I believe you. Why don't we get together tonight for a drink?" She was still concentrating on her sketch.

I hesitated and she turned toward me. "See ... I told you so."

"No … No … tonight's fine. I'm sorry. I can't explain why, but I'm being very cautious right now." It wasn't a lie. It just wasn't all of the truth.

"The divorce?" She had gone back to her sketch.

"Something like that."

"Cheer up, Lee. You'll get over it. The statistics are in your favor." She said it with a smile in her voice.

I was pretty sure I was sunk. My plan for three days of celibacy looked pretty dim. She was coming on strong and she wasn't in the mood to take no for an answer. On the other hand, she was gorgeous. I had often fantasized about tall women and here is one being delivered to me. It was that "gift horse" thing again. Ah, what the hell. Who was it going to harm?

"So … how long are you up here for?" I asked.

"A week. It's one of my vacation weeks and Brian is away on business, so I get a week of peace."

A week with this woman would be a challenge. "Where are you staying?"

"I've got a time share that I use for a month each year. This is week two."

"It's a lovely area. I can see why you'd like it."

"What are you doing for dinner?" she asked. Nothing like being direct and to the point, I thought.

"Ahhhh … nothing special. I'm here on my own."

"Good … why don't you let me feed you?"

Well, I thought in resignation, I might as well just surrender. "That's very kind of you. I'd love to join you," I said without really realizing my double entendre.

I thought I heard her snort, but I wasn't sure. "I'm just about done. We can walk back to our cars together if you like."

"Fine."

She packed up her little kit and put it in a small backpack and slung it over her shoulder. She was wearing a light cotton t-shirt in pale green with an art design on the front. Her lovely breasts made sure I couldn't see all of the design. Her shorts were snug and the long, perfectly tapered legs that fell from her fabulous hips were on full display. She had a slight tan from somewhere. Although today was an unusually warm day for this time of year, the tan wouldn't have come from here.

We strolled together down the meadow toward the cars. She seemed to be happy to be close to me and I didn't discourage her. I was going to bask in the company of this woman just as I had relished the company of the others I had met this past week. If I couldn't control it, I might as well just surrender and enjoy it. If it was a fantasy, it was my fantasy, and a damn fine one at that.

When we reached the cars, she told me where her condo was and suggested I come over at seven. I smiled my agreement and said I would see her then. As I slipped into my car, I realized I hadn't touched her other than the brief handshake when we met. I had a suspicion that would be corrected this evening. I began to imagine just what this woman would look like naked and in my arms. I had reason to believe I would find out tonight.

When I arrived at Beth's just before seven, I was surprised at how nice her condo was. It was clearly a cut above the ordinary. I wondered how she could afford something this elegant. From our conversation this afternoon, I got the impression she didn't have anyone as a steady boyfriend.

When she opened the door, I'm sure my jaw dropped. She was wearing a low cut, black top sprinkled with small reflecting bits that would be dazzling if it weren't for the competition from her cleavage. Her skirt was the same tightly packaged gray wool from the previous evening. She was barefoot, and I wondered if that was for me or just for comfort. She looked fantastic. The hair, the eyes, the freckles, the breasts, and the long legs. It was damned unfair. She had her share of looks and a few others' share as well. I was getting that swell feeling in my pants. You know the one -- the one that sometimes you try to hide and other times you try to show.

She wore that lovely smile and I felt very welcome. I followed her into the living room and my opinion of the outside was reinforced by the inside. This was one classy place. The finest in modern furnishings, hardwood floors decorated with what appeared to be Persian rugs, decor featuring crystal and various objet d'art, as well as paintings hung in strategic places. In other words, high rent! This didn't seem to be the playground for a personal assistant, but what did I know. This was out of my league.

"I'm impressed. This is quite the spectacular place. Not what I would have expected," I said in admiration.

"Well, it's not mine. I just get to use it. It belongs to a guy who has the hots for me," she laughed.

"So, what's the problem? I thought you intimidated men."

"Well ... this is different. He's married and he won't be leaving her anytime soon. It's her money," she said in a nonchalant tone.

"Ah hah! Just as I thought, a kept woman," I laughed.

She laughed with me. It was obviously not a sensitive issue with her. "Well, we all have our failings, Lee."

"I'm having real trouble with the idea that you intimidate men, or that it interferes with your relationships with men. You are a very beautiful woman and I can't believe you haven't got a boatload of guys banging on your door."

"Well, I wish it were so, but it isn't. Maybe I'm hard to handle. Maybe my standards are too high. Maybe I'm just unlucky. Who knows?"

Never let it be said that I was shy. "So, I guess you have to decide whether I can meet your standards or whether you just got lucky," I said with my newly acquired self-confidence.

"Not so fast, buster. We haven't had dinner yet," she smirked.

"Point taken. Lead me to your kitchen."

She strolled -- and I do mean strolled -- into the kitchen area and it was just as elegant and modern as the rest of the condo. A restaurant-sized stove and oven, a meat-locker-sized refrigerator/freezer and everything in stainless steel. There was food on the island and food on the counter and she was serious about cooking dinner. I surveyed the fixings and determined that this was no ordinary meat and potatoes dinner. I spotted some fresh, hand-peeled shrimp, a loin of lamb and the some sort of special rice dish. There were fresh green beans and assorted other vegetables on a separate plate. I smiled to myself, knowing that I was going to be well fed.

I was right, of course. There was no reason to doubt it. It's just the way things had been ordained in the past week. I was getting an erection just thinking of how well things were progressing. Beth was spectacular and I was bulletproof. What was left to chance? Nothing!

So, imagine my surprise when we had dinner, some wine, a lovely light dessert, a long, interesting conversation about a variety of topics and then ... she said it was time for me to say goodnight! What the hell? This isn't the normal script. I have to go? Well, considering all the other crazy things that had happened in the past week, why should I be surprised? I accepted my fate reluctantly, but acted like a man and kissed her cheek, thanked her profusely for the wonderful dinner, and said I hoped to see her again.

I drove back to my B & B in a state of mild shock. Perhaps I was being unrealistic. Perhaps this past week had given me delusions of grandeur. Perhaps I had screwed up with Beth. I didn't think so, and she didn't seem to indicate anything was amiss, but I wasn't so sure. What about all that byplay in the afternoon and at the condo? As I let myself into my room, I realized I didn't have her phone number. I knew where she was and I knew she would be there until next weekend, but that might be a bit awkward. Hmmm? This was a switch.

I slept fitfully that night. I had dreams about a naked Beth and a number of positions I could imagine myself being in as I made love to her. Unfortunately, they were just dreams. I recognized that I was committed to seducing her, or at least letting her seduce me. Whatever worked! So much for my celibacy. Screw that! I wanted Beth and I was going to let my new-found powers help me.

I had my usual good appetite the next morning and once again, I overindulged at breakfast. I was tempted to head back up to the meadow and see if Beth was there. It was a reasonable possibility with another sunny, spring day ahead. I decided against it however. I had only one more night to achieve my temporary celibacy goal, and Beth would be here for the rest of the week. I had checked with the hostess, and my room would be available until Thursday if I wanted to extend my stay. I told her I would let her know tomorrow morning.

I decided on a day trip up the highway to Radium Hot Springs. Despite the fact that it was an overly-popular tourist spot, I had fond memories of Radium from my childhood. It was a regular stop for our family on our way back from visiting the grandparents in Calgary. It was only a few minutes drive from Fairmont, and I set off at mid-morning. I spent the rest of the morning wandering around the old haunt, had a light snack for lunch, enjoyed a glass of wine in the early spring sunshine, and finally, just after three o'clock, got back into my car and turned back toward Fairmont.

I would be passing the road to the meadow where Beth had been sketching, and I toyed with the idea of checking to see if she was there. It was a mental coin toss, and by the time I approached the cut-off to the old road I had decided I would check the place out. I drove up the rough track slowly and I wasn't really surprised that her SUV was parked in the same spot as yesterday. I got out, considered my options, looked at my watch, shrugged my shoulders, and began walking up the incline toward where she was yesterday.

Don't have to walk very far. She was just over the rise of the first hill, and this time she was sitting on a small stool and had an easel in front of her. She was obviously painting in the scene she had sketched yesterday. Again, I don't want to startle her, so I moved out wide to give her some warning that I was near. She must have picked me up fairly quickly as I saw her head turn and look toward me. She was wearing a wide brimmed straw hat and a different shorts and t-shirt outfit from yesterday. She looked just as dazzling today as she did then.

She waved in recognition and then turned back to her painting as I walked toward her.

"I wondered if you'd come looking for me."

"It was a coin toss."

"Who won?"

"I did, of course," I chuckled.

"Figures." She hadn't looked away from her painting the entire time I had been there and she was concentrating on something, making sure it was just right. I looked at what she had done so far and it looked very good and very professional. I decided to remain quiet while she worked.

"I brought my own water this time. Would you like some?" she asked.

"Thanks, I'm fine for now."

"So I guess this means you really aren't intimidated by me."

"I guess."

"Wanna do dinner again?"

"Sure ... why not?"

"Wanna fool around later?"

"Sure ... why not?" I repeated. She had this way with words; an economical and to-the-point way.

"Can you cook?" She still hadn't turned away from her painting.

"Yup."

"Good."

"Are you going to be here for a while yet?"

"Nope. Light's going and I'm getting stiff. I'll be done in two minutes."

"I'll stick around and give you a hand with your gear."

"Thanks."

We walked together down the slope of the meadow toward our vehicles, chatting about our day.

"Do you paint only landscapes?" I asked.

"Pretty much. I'm not very good at human forms. They are very complex and I don't seem to be able to get them just right for my own satisfaction."

"I remember being in a modern art gallery a while back," I began. "There was a painting;,quite bold colors and very impressionistic. It wasn't a large canvas, but there was a form ... a woman's form. It was just three or four lines on the canvas, but it was the unmistakable outline of a beautiful woman. No face, no arms, just a form. I've never forgotten it."

"If I could paint like that, I would have been in that gallery too. It's what separates real artists from hobbyists like me."

"I like your work ... or at least what I've seen of it," I said quickly.

"A half finished canvas isn't much to see."

"What I could see ... I was impressed. You have talent ... but I get the impression you don't like to take chances," I said carefully.

"What makes you say that?"

"Your subjects ... no danger ... no risk ... pleasant pictures of pleasant scenes. I hope that doesn't offend you."

She stopped and turned to me. "So ... in your opinion, what should I be painting?"

"Things that frighten you. Things that challenge you. Things that threaten you. Things that are difficult?" I was speaking with more boldness than I felt.

"You've got some pretty strong opinions."

"Yeah … sorry. I'm used to seeing a lot of artwork. My father is an artist … or at least he was."

"Was?"

"Early onset Parkinson's Disease."

"Oh … I'm sorry. What kind of art did he produce?"

"He was an illustrator. Mostly black on white, with brush."

She looked at me and then a puzzled look came over her. "Is your father Gordon Stephenson?"

"Yes."

"He's brilliant. I love his work. I have two of his prints in my home," she gushed. "You must be very proud."

"Yes. I admire his talent. Unfortunately, it isn't hereditary."

"Yeah … I know. My mother is a musician. I haven't got a musical bone in my body."

"Ah … art … music … they come under the heading of special talents. They are all gifts to be nurtured and developed," I said pompously.

"Very deep … very perceptive. I've decided. You can stay." She was laughing at me.

"Thanks … so long as you understand that I just gave you a classic example of bullshit baffles brains."

"Yeah … but it was high quality bullshit," she laughed again.

"Can't fool you … can I?"

"Oh hell… keep trying … that's the fun of it."

It was a light and fun conversation that we were both enjoying. This was a bright and very alive woman. Her physical presence and charm were obvious, but her mind was always working, and based on our conversation last night, and the bit of byplay this afternoon, she could hold her own in any company. She was a worthy opponent and a treat to be with.

I returned to the elegant condo at seven as requested, and Beth let me in. She was wearing another of her tantalizing outfits that did nothing to quell my interest or my libido. It took a moment, but after I watched her move through the living room, I was sure she wasn't wearing a bra. I immediately wondered what else she wasn't wearing.

I had taken the precaution of including some condoms in my pocket in case the need arose. I thought for a moment that this was a bit of conceit on my part, but I ended up rationalizing it as just being prepared. After all, just what would "fool around" mean if not what I had expected the previous evening?

"You wanted me to cook?" I reminded her.

"It's nice tonight. Not too cool. I thought we'd use the barbeque."

"Fine. What would you like me to do?"

"I haven't decided. I've got some steaks, some albacore tuna, and some chicken. Everything is fresh."

"How about the tuna?"

"Sounds good. Won't take long, either. I'll toss some salad and I have some of last night's rice I can heat in the microwave. Does that sound alright?"

"Great. Do you have a white wine to go with it?"

She produced a nice Chardonnay and I opened it for her while I waited for the grill to heat up. The tuna would take only a couple of minutes to cook. I had some time to think about what sort of seduction I could employ on this interesting Amazon of a woman. I probably am not going to have to work very hard if our conversation of this afternoon was any indication. I was having those thoughts again of what it would be like to be locked in an embrace with Beth, both of us naked. It was getting pretty good at visualizing my more lurid thoughts.

We enjoyed the dinner, and I helped her with the few dishes we needed to clean by hand while the rest went into the dishwasher. Our conversation continued to be easy and interesting, and I found Beth to be a delight to be around. She wasn't just easy on the eyes, she was full of interesting ideas and she had an amazing general knowledge. I had always admired my dad's general knowledge and tried to emulate him, and Beth was very well informed by any standard.

We adjourned to the living room with the last of the Chardonnay and sat together on the sofa. There wasn't much distance between us, but I decided to let Beth make the first move. Well, that's what I thought, anyway. As it turned out, there wasn't any move. We just sat there talking about inconsequential things, now and then interrupted by periods of silence. Finally, I couldn't stand it any more.

"Beth ... can you give me a clue about what you expect from me?" I asked in a somewhat plaintive voice.

It was a straightforward question and caught her by surprise. "What do you mean?"

"Well ... let's see. Yesterday, you made it pretty clear that you were interested in me and then ... poof! I went home with a feeling that I had upset you or badly misread you. Then, this afternoon, I clearly remember you asking me if I'd like to fool around. So here we are and we seem to be stuck in neutral." I tried very hard not to sound accusatory or upset. I wasn't sure if it worked.

"Got you confused, have I?" she grinned.

"Oh yeah."

"Well ... yesterday was a dirty trick of nature. My period didn't end as I expected. Sorry, but I didn't have the courage to tell you."

"That explains last night," I said carefully. "So, where do we go from here?"

"Hmmmm ... let's see. Since you didn't think much of my painting, maybe I should just boot you out again." She was poking me lightly with her finger in mock approbation.

"Just how did I give you that impression?"

"Don't you remember? No danger! No risks!"

"Ah ... well ... you shouldn't take the criticism of the unskilled as serious comment. I suppose I was thinking of the work of a friend of my father's when I said that. He did landscapes and old buildings, barns and old houses and the like. His wife died of cancer when he was still in his fifties. He was devastated by her death and I remember my father showing me a painting he had done after she had died. There was no mistaking his mood and his feelings. It left an indelible impression on me. All his other paintings were nice pictures of old buildings or well composed country scenes. This one was special. It was his soul, torn open for everyone to see. It took his wife's death to release that emotion onto his canvas."

Beth didn't say anything for a few moments. She stared at me and then looked away with a wrinkled brow. I wondered if I had pushed too far, been too blunt. Who was I to criticize an artist when I was completely without talent myself? I was just relating an event, I rationalized ... a very personal one.

"I haven't ever had anything that traumatic happen in my life," she finally said in a quiet voice. "The worst thing that's ever happened to me was when a boyfriend broke up with me in high school, just before the spring prom. I thought I was going to die, but I got over it. "

"Ever try to paint a self-portrait?" I asked.

"No ... never." She looked at me again. "Why? Do you think I should?"

"Why not try. A self-portrait means the only person you can offend is yourself," I suggested. "I think the thing that separates true artists from the rest of us is their ego, their ability to be self-centered. It doesn't apply just to painters, but sculptors, architects, actors, musicians, opera singers; all the great ones have big egos and the courage to stick their necks out in public. Sometimes you need to be selfish and please only yourself. To hell with what anyone else thinks."

She looked at me for a moment and then a smile began to invade her face. "I was told you were shy. I find that hard to believe."

"I am. I was. I'm not so sure about myself anymore."

"So what was the traumatic event in your life?" she asked with genuine curiosity.

"The day I discovered that I wasn't in love with my wife and that I probably never had been," I said almost automatically. It was true and it was painful, and it had been with me every day since I had realized that truth.

"Do you think of it as lost time in your life? Wasted time, I mean."

"No ... I don't think so. I had a companion and a friend and there was ... intimacy. I don't think I knew what love was. I'm still not sure I do. I don't think I've ever known it, so how would I compare?"

"I know what you mean," Beth said sympathetically. "I don't know what it is either. I hope I will someday soon. I think we all need it in our lives to make us complete, but I have this feeling that not so many people really find it. True, undying love, I mean."

"You're young yet. Barely thirty? There's time. You just have to follow your instincts. It's like that artist attitude I mentioned. You have to be selfish enough that you won't settle for anything less than the real thing."

"Have you got a degree in philosophy or something?" she kidded.

"Naw. Just a few years on you and some real-life experiences to draw on."

I felt good about being with Beth. She was interesting, inarguably beautiful, and a very self-aware young woman. However, she had doubts about herself that seemed misplaced. She was too self-conscious about her height and self-deprecating about her artistic talent. I wondered idly if she ever got angry about anything. I decided not to try and find out. I reached out for her upper arm and pulled her toward me. She didn't resist and in a moment, we were locked in an embrace, kissing and dueling with our tongues.

Her hand dropped to my crotch, and she was searching for my soon-to-be full erection. The touch of her hand through my pants was more than enough to bring my cock to full attention.

She pulled back for a moment with a smile on her lips. "You've been fantasizing about this, haven't you?"

"Absolutely! Several times in several ways."

"Oh … are you ready to show me the ways?"

"As long as you're ready, I'm ready." I untangled myself and helped her to her feet. She led me toward what I presumed was the bedroom and along the way, I surveyed her clothes to determine how best to rid her of them. It appeared to be a one piece outfit, tied with a sash. It was shiny satin, turquoise green in color, and I suspected she might be naked beneath it.

The bedroom was no less spectacular than the other rooms. A king size bed in a wrought iron frame was centered on one wall of the room. The floor was a deep cherry wood, as were the furnishings. Three white throw rugs surrounded the bed on each side, and at the foot. Two glass and wrought iron tables took the place of night stands. There were no drawers or hiding places for any items, toys or otherwise.

Beth turned toward me and I stepped forward, reaching for the sash of her outfit. I pulled it gently and it undid easily, allowing the top of the one piece garment to open and reveal her remarkable breasts. She was a fantasy come to life; a large, voluptuous woman who exuded sexuality from every pore. My hands slipped up across her breasts, allowing my palms to rub against her nipples, but not stopping until I had reached her shoulders. I pushed the light fabric away and was rewarded with the shiny, green garment falling to the floor. Without taking her eyes from mine, she stepped out of the puddle of satin at her feet and moved toward the bed, completely naked.

There is no known way for a man to undress in an erotic manner when he is wearing conventional men's clothing. It just can't be done. Beth sat on the bed with a bemused look, watching me fumble with my shirt, pants, socks and finally, shorts. At last, we were on equal terms and I joined her on the bed, sitting beside her and stroking her breasts and tummy softly with my hands. She leaned into me and we kissed; at first tentatively, and then more passionately. She reached for my cock, now almost erect, and held it in her hand, squeezing it slightly.

I allowed my hand to slip further down and began to probe her neatly trimmed mound. I used my forefinger to begin the stroking of her labial lips, and as they moistened I pushed my finger into her as slowly and as smoothly as I could. She began to respond. She hung her head on my shoulder, and I could hear her breath become more irregular. I could feel her hips begin to move rhythmically as I continued masturbating her with my finger. I added a second finger, curling upward with the first and began a search for her G spot. I was sure I had found it when she began to react more dramatically to my probing.

It was at that point that Beth began to take over. She grabbed my cock, pushed my active hand out of the way and climbed on top of me, stuffing my erection into her with a single stab. The next thing I knew, she had a lock on my shoulders as she pounded up and down on my cock, her eyes merely slits and with a grimace on her lips. This was apparently serious business to her, and she was relentless as she used me for her own needs. Some might call it selfish, but I was more inclined to think of it as reckless.

I wasn't hesitant to join in on the "fun," but she was in a world of her own, driving herself to some orgasm as yet unclaimed. I had no idea how long I could hold on under this assault, but it was strangely non-erotic, and I found I was just a passenger at this point. I really didn't feel that I was close to letting go, so I just held on with both hands and let her do her "thing."

I'm not sure how long it lasted, but it was far longer than I expected, and when she finally reached her destination, she redefined the meaning of "explosive orgasm." I'm sure the ground really did shake. Her body collapsed on mine and she was gasping for breath at a furious rate. I just held her until things started to return to normal, and she could at least say a few words between her attempts to take in more air.

"See what I mean?" she finally managed.

"That was pretty crazy. Was that normal?"

"Only when I've been without for a while. Once you get me started, I'm hard to stop." She was nuzzled into my neck and had returned to a more passive state.

"Tell me what I can do for you, then. I'm here to please you," I said with some trepidation.

"Baby, I like it all. You can't think of anything that I won't enjoy."

I decided to go back to basics. I'd rely on my old, reliable top to bottom tongue and finger work and just see where it took us. I rolled her over on her back and I began to make love to her spectacular breasts, using my tongue, lips and fingertips. At first, nothing seemed to be happening to her, but it didn't take long before I was getting vocal signals and body movement that told me I was on the right track.

I rose up slightly to begin my move down her fabulous body, and she promptly pushed her hand down my abdomen and grasped my cock. Now, this could be a problem. There was only so much distance between the length of her arm and the length of my cock, and I wasn't going to slipping down anywhere as long as she had this grip on my manhood.

"Beth … let go of me. Let me do my thing for a while. I'm not going anywhere. I'll be right here when you need me," I promised.

She released me and sighed as her hand returned and joined her other hand on the back of my head. My tongue in her navel cavity sparked a brief response, but as I suspected she was into more direct contact, so I continued my way down to her lovely pussy. It was bright red from the violent exercise it had suffered a few moments earlier, and her clitoris was still extended and prominent. I decided to wait until I had paid more attention to the lower extremities and I pushed her thighs wide apart as I moved further down.

I began my assault by dragging the top of my tongue slowly along her perineum and upward toward her labia, stopping just before I reached her clit. She pushed her hips up in response to my strokes and as she did, I moved one hand to her ass cheek and began to slip a finger inside the crack and gently touch her anus. She jumped in response to my first touch, telling me I had found a sensitive spot. I kept sliding my finger across and around the tiny opening as my tongue continued its slow glide up her lovely pussy.

I kept this up for several moments until, without any warning, I began to insert my fingertip into her anus. She reacted again, but this time with a vocal grunt that I took for approval. Each time that I stroked her with my tongue, I pushed my finger slightly farther into her ass. It was clearly with her approval as she began to move her hips again in that very inviting way. It was time to push the process along, and again, without warning, I locked my lips on her clit and began stroking my finger in and out of her ass. She responded quickly with a howl of surprise and then began pushing back on my hand as I finger fucked her ass. All the while, my tongue was massaging her clit as I held it between my lips.

She was really starting to move now. I added a second finger in her ass and she arched her back violently in response and then continued her pushing back. I had released her clit, and brought my head up as her hips were reacting wildly again. I took it as an invitation to complete this portion of my foreplay by adding a third finger in her ass and increasing the pace of my stroke.

"Awwwwwh gawwwd," she howled. Her breathing was back to gasps and her hips fairly danced above the bed and my hand moved rapidly in and out of her ass. Suddenly, she grabbed my wrist and pulled my hand away from her and then rolled over, sticking her formidable butt in the air.

"Give me the real thing … now!" she demanded.

I crabbed up behind her, lubricated my erection in her pussy and then pushed the head of my cock into the now-widened anal opening. I was careful and applied a steady push as I entered her. Beth was groaning and gasping, but pushing back at me as well, welcoming my invasion. Soon I was almost halfway in and I began to pull back and then forward slowly, allowing her to get used to my stroke. I had never done this before and I was going on instinct and caution as I began my first anal intercourse.

Beth was no rookie at this, and within a few strokes she was demanding more depth and faster strokes.

"Come on, Lee ... fuck my ass! Give it to me! Make me come!" She almost shouted her encouragement.

I wondered how long I would last and the answer was – not long. Fortunately, I think Beth was ready as well, and when I felt myself about to let go, I told her so.

"Here it comes, Beth. Here it comes ... I can't hold back." And I didn't. I felt the warm spurts of semen in her tight anal canal. It was a whole, new thing. It was completely different than vaginal sex and I hoped she felt rewarded.

"Oh God, Lee. That was great. Oh, I love the feel of come in my ass. It feels so good ... so good," she sighed as she began to collapse on her stomach.

I slipped out of her and lay beside her with my arm over her back. She turned her head toward me and she had a nice smile.

"You were great, Lee. I'm feeling real good about you in my bed. You were great." She raised her head and moved toward me and kissed me. "Are you finished for tonight?" she asked quietly.

"Do you want me to be finished?"

"No!" she said abruptly, her head popping up with a surprised look on her face. "No, I want you to stay. I want as much of you as I can have for as long as I can have it." She was serious. It wasn't just pillow talk. She wanted all I could give her and I was wondering just how much I could give.

"I'm not Superman. I'll do the best I can for you."

"Hmmmm. I have a feeling that you'll be just fine. Right now, I think we should take a break, have a shower and maybe a glass of wine or brandy, and then, when we're both ready, we can come back here. I'll change the sheets while you're in the shower and you can pour the wine when I'm in there. Okay?"

"Okay," I said with some disappointment.

"What's the matter?"

"I was hoping to have that shower with you. I can always help you change the sheets."

"Offer accepted," she smiled. She slipped from the bed and strolled toward the ensuite. I followed and we entered what must have been the giant economy size shower enclosure. The walls were sheathed in large, random shaped slate with a dark, tiled floor. Several stainless steel controls were on the wall along with several shower outlets. Beth pushed a single button and the shower heads sprang to life, apparently with a pre-set water temperature.

As I lathered and washed this incredible woman, my cock was growing again and I thought for a moment, we might have a session in the shower.

"Save it for later," she said with a smile. "You're going to need it."

I could hardly be disappointed. I was living out another of these almost expected fantasies, and my only duty was not to screw it up.

We had fun drying each other with her big, soft towels and soon, dressed in a matching pair of terrycloth robes, we were in the kitchen, sipping wine, and nibbling on snacks that Beth had previously prepared. I found myself staring at her. I could understand how she could overwhelm a man. It wasn't just a matter of size, but a matter of her aggressive sexual appetite. She was a tiger in bed, and I wondered how any man could keep up with her over the long haul. On the other hand, she was so incredibly beautiful, so irresistible. No red-blooded heterosexual man could resist her.

It was about an hour later that we returned to the bedroom, and this time Beth touched a control panel on the wall, and the lights dimmed to a very low level and soft music played in the background. This was a much more sensual atmosphere and it prefaced a much more controlled and sensuous encounter. It was a flip side of Beth Jorgenson, and I was greatly relieved. I was back where I thought I could participate, and not just be a person along for the ride.

I moved behind her, undid the sash on her robe, and smoothly removed it from her. She turned and did the same for me. She pulled back the sheets of the remade bed and slipped inside, inviting me to join her. I slid in beside her and thus began one of the most erotic episodes of my life.

I have no real recollection of how it all began or when it all ended. Suffice it to say, it was a continuum of sexual pleasing for both of us. It lacked the reckless abandon of our first encounter, but it was far more satisfying. We took our time and enjoyed every minute of it. We tried many positions and loved all of them. Beth was very intuitive when it came to prolonging my performance, and I was very grateful for that. Under other circumstances, it might have been over within a few minutes and I would have been denied the most satisfying time I could ever have conjured in my dreams.

I had a hard time figuring out what Beth was all about. She was very sexual, and I've already extolled the virtues of her beauty. What I couldn't figure out was her apparent inability to find a permanent relationship, even a semi-permanent one. Once I got past the initial thermonuclear blast, she was the picture of erotic self-control. It made not the slightest difference in the enjoyment we shared. She responded to my various teasings and gentle torments with vocal and body expressions which told me that she was totally appreciative of my efforts. We were a fine match.

At some point, it all ended quietly, and I awoke the next morning holding her closely to me in the spoon position. She exuded that wonderful scent women produce first thing in the morning, and my cock was at full attention. A short time later, she began to awaken. She couldn't help but notice my condition, since it was nestled comfortably between the cheeks of her glorious ass. I heard her purr her comfort and we remained as we were for several minutes until she turned toward me.

"Good morning," she said sleepily.

"Good morning. Did you sleep well?"

"Ummmh. Yeah. Fine." She sounded uncertain. "You wore me out," she added.

"I did?" That's the last thing I expected to hear from her. I thought it was the other way around. I pulled her closer to me just to emphasize how happy I was just to hold her.

It didn't take long to figure out that she had fallen back asleep, and I quietly slipped out of bed and headed for the shower. I remembered which button she had pushed and sure enough, the multi-head shower started up and within seconds it was cascading warm water over my tired frame. I washed and lingered under the spray for several minutes before I got out and dried myself. I poked around in the drawers and came up with a disposable razor and some shaving gel and cleaned up my face.

I walked out of the ensuite and saw that Beth was still fast asleep. I tied the robe around me and headed for the kitchen. A brief search produced some juice, a bagel, coffee for the machine, and even some dry cereal. I poured some orange juice and made a pot of coffee. I toasted the bagel and took it into the living room with my coffee and turned on the TV to check the news.

I was on my second cup when Beth appeared in the living room and sat beside me on the sofa.

"Hi," I said, turning to her. "Can I get you something?"

"Coffee … please."

I got up and went into the kitchen, found a mug and poured the coffee. I remembered she didn't take cream or sugar from the other night, so I brought the hot, steaming mug back to the living room and placed it on the coffee table in front of her. She hadn't moved a muscle since she had plunked herself down on the sofa and I wasn't even sure if she was fully conscious.

"You okay?" I asked.

"Hmmmm. Just tired," she finally responded. "I thought you said you weren't Superman."

I might have had a grin on my face when I said, "I'm not. I gather you weren't disappointed."

"I may not be able to walk for a couple of days," she said without smiling.

"Sorry. I didn't think I was that rough."

Beth turned and looked at me. "You weren't." She sounded reassuring. "I just got carried away and you were strong enough to stay with me. I didn't expect that."

"Neither did I."

"Surprise! When do you have to check out of your room?"

"Today."

"Why don't you move in here? I have the rest of the week and I'd be grateful for the company."

I really didn't have to think very hard about it. "Sure." It was another of those fascinating opportunities I was being presented out of the blue.

"Good. Why don't you check out and bring your things here. Maybe by the time you get back, I'll be awake," she said with a tired smile.

Well, there goes the best of my intentions again. I managed two nights without sex. Actually, I can only take credit for one since I was quite prepared to bed her the night before last, and only the dreaded curse stopped me. However, one has to accept one's limitations, or in my case, uncontrolled destiny. I happily packed my bag, paid my bill, and headed back to the condo, stopping briefly to pick up some Astroglide at the local drug store. I was concerned for Beth's comfort.

When I returned to the condo, Beth was looking considerably more alert. She had showered, dressed, and eaten, and she greeted me at the door with a lovely big kiss and a bum squeeze. Very considerate!

It had started to rain and looked like the next day or so would be at least cloudy with scattered showers. That could be the perfect excuse for us to stay indoors. We did a lot of touching and holding that afternoon. Beth spent most of the day with a dreamy smile on her face and I guess I didn't look much different. It was one of the after-effects that left you feeling so superior and so satisfied that you couldn't find the words to express it. I tried. I opened my laptop and tried to record what had happened, but I failed. I might as well have attempted to describe Mona Lisa's smile.

We spent the next day indoors too. I encouraged Beth to try a self-portrait and she gave it a good effort. After several of what she thought were failed attempts, I asked her what she thought was wrong with them.

"I don't exactly know. They just don't look right to me. They don't look like I think I look. Does that make sense?" she asked.

"Yes … in a way. But, are you looking for a literal translation or is there something you want to show others about yourself?

She looked at me with a strange, wrinkled grimace. "I don't know. How do I look to you?"

"Literally, you're physically a very beautiful woman. But what I see sometimes, is a very insecure woman, uncertain of who she is and what she is looking for in her life." I hoped I am not being too brash or aggressive with my comments. From what I had seen of her sketches, she saw a different woman than I did. I was trying to tell her that.

"Why don't you try a mask," I suggested. "It doesn't have to be literal and usually they are less complex in execution than real faces. They don't have all the subtlety and nuance of the human face." I had done my best to plant the seed of alternatives. It was up to Beth to find a way to express herself. I had the feeling that once she found that way, she would be excited with the results. She needed to be patient with herself and persistent with her experiments.

"You're full of ideas, aren't you?" I think she was enjoying my contribution and encouragement.

"I'm full of something." I was laughing. Talk about conceited! Me, giving artist ideas!

I went back to my journal and before I knew it, it was almost six in the afternoon. I stood up, stretched and walked into the spare bedroom to see how Beth had made out. As I walked into the room, the easel was facing toward her with the light coming in over her shoulder and I couldn't see what she had done unless I moved behind her. Beth had her brush in her hand and was studying something on the canvas with great concentration.

I walked behind her quietly and looked at what she had done. I was amazed. It was like nothing she had done before. It was stunning; a surrealistic expression of a human face. Whose face, I could not tell. I couldn't even tell which sex. But it was amazing. It was bold, not just with the brush strokes, but with color as well. I was trying to determine what the expression on "its" face could be. It looked forbidding and yet, not angry. It had power. I was curious about what Beth was trying to say. I didn't dare interrupt her though.

"There's another drying in the closet, Lee," she said, still concentrating on the canvas in front of her.

I walked to the closet and looked in. There was another canvas, sitting on the floor, propped up against the back wall. I squatted down to have a closer look. It was another mask in stark black and white. It was almost like a theatre mask, but more expressive. Again, it had an enigmatic expression. It was impressive as well.

"These are wonderful, Beth." I meant it. They were so completely different and so foreign to her usual style. She had broken out of her comfort zone and created something completely new.

"Yeah … it's crazy, but I think I like them. They are so different, I don't know what to make of them, even though I painted them myself. It was almost 'stream of consciousness' painting. I didn't even sketch anything more than the outline shape. I just let the brush go where it wanted to."

She was almost giggling with excitement. She had found something new and she was pumped at the discovery. I couldn't help but smile. It would be interesting to see where this would take her. It might be just a hobby, but she had prodigious talent. It was just a matter of finding the vehicle for her expression. I felt really happy for her.

I stayed with her for the rest of the week and I don't think Beth spent more than a couple of hours that she wasn't either painting, eating, or together with me in bed. Her excitement with her art carried over into the bedroom, and I was treated to a festival of fornication. If there is a sexual equivalent to a gourmand, I was perilously close to meeting that dubious standard.

All good things must come to an end, however. On Saturday night, Beth and I packed our bags in preparation for her early departure the next morning. Vancouver would be a long drive for her, whereas I had no particular destination. I was sad to see it end.

"Will you be coming back to Vancouver?" she asked as I prepared to depart.

"Yes. I'll probably have a job there at some point."

"Will I see you again?" Her eyes were searching mine.

"Yes. That's a definite yes," I smiled before kissing her soundly.

She was a magnificent woman with a world of artistic talent just waiting to be discovered. She had five very good paintings to take home with her. In the meantime, she had a job that would keep her in groceries even if it didn't give her the personal satisfaction she craved. For my part, I was just happy I got to spend some time with her. I wouldn't forget her soon.

Part 5 – Pattie:

"Don't move. Stay right where you are," I whispered.

She complied as I felt her muscles relax and her body slump against my chest. We were silent. There was no need for conversation. We had both exclaimed our enjoyment over the past half hour and swam in the pleasure of our shared passion. We had expressed our fulfillment at the completion of a blissful union.

We lay there in the dark, the gentle rocking of the boat adding to our peaceful recovery. I pulled the comforter over us to ward off the chill beginning to seep into the cabin as nightfall became complete. A purr of satisfaction was mumbled into my chest as the lovely young woman tried to worm her way even further into my body.

"I could stay here forever," she murmured.

"Uhmmm," I agreed.

My hands roamed over the naked body of my partner, touching gently with my fingertips as I stroked the back of her thighs, across her perfect, round ass, finishing lightly on her spinal column. I could sense her reactions in my chest and abdomen as she responded to my touches.

"I've never been fucked on a boat before," she mumbled.

"Likewise," I chuckled.

"I feel very good, very … happy." Her muffled voice echoed the sentiment.

"What did you say your real name was?" She sounded half asleep.

"Leighton."

"Sir Leighton … my white knight. Thanks for saving me." Her voice was fading as she slipped further down the path toward slumber.

"You're welcome. Now get some sleep." It wasn't an order, but she didn't take much convincing. She was out within seconds.

As the lovely, mysterious young woman snored lightly against my chest, my thoughts drifted back to how all this had come to pass.

Weary from driving and exploring back roads, I had stopped in Sicamous for lunch yesterday. As I got out of the Subaru and stretched my cramped limbs, I noticed a large, new houseboat being loaded on a railroad flatcar. I stood and watched for a while as I regained my equilibrium. I looked about at the little lakeside town and decided it would do for my next destination.

My survey detected a large sign for houseboat rentals in the next block. I had forgotten how popular they were on Shushwap Lake, and decided I would look into it after I had eaten.

The Lakeside Bistro satisfied my lust for a greasy burger and fries, topped off with a decent strawberry milkshake. This was clearly a new definition for bistro. It was a retro-lunch counter if there ever was one. I paid the aging waitress, left a two dollar tip and sauntered out onto the street. The lunch was sitting in a lump in the bottom of my stomach, warning me not to make any sudden moves.

I strolled slowly down the street toward the houseboat rental office, and was about to open the front door when I noticed the sign in the window. *Closed for lunch. Back at 1.* I looked at my watch and saw I had a half hour to kill. A few yards away, a lane led to the water and access to a dock where a half-dozen houseboats were tied up. Might as well have a look, I thought.

Since it was just me, I wouldn't need a big boat. There were two craft that looked to be in the mid-twenties in length and that would be more than enough. I peeked into the windows to get a look at the layout and soon determined I was looking at a floating camper. The cabinets, kitchen, bathroom, and folding bed/lounges were the same as a dozen different campers I had seen.

The superstructure was mounted on a flat platform with two aluminum pontoons and an outboard motor nested in the center of the stern. A two-station mechanical steering system was linked to the motor. It is simple, but effective and can easily be handled by one person. A small command bridge and an inboard wheelhouse for poor weather made it suitable for my purposes. I was interested in doing a bit of exploration around the popular lake, and since it was pre-season, I might even get a discount rate. The six boats tied to the dock indicated they weren't overwhelmed with customers.

"Hi … can I help you?" It was a woman's voice. A young woman. I pushed myself back from my scan of the boat's interior and turned to the source of the question.

"Hi … just looking. Thinking of renting one," I explained, squinting into the bright sun reflecting off the glassy lake.

I looked the woman over as my eyes began to adjust. She was attractive, possibly mid-twenties, dressed in a black tank top and black shorts with black sneakers. Her left shoulder sported a large, multicolored tattoo of indeterminate design. It was partly masked by her developing tan. It was still early in June.

She appeared to be of average height and build, but her hips and ass however, were something else. They looked very mature, very round, and very lush.

"You work here?"

"Yeah … for now," she answered economically.

"OK then … tell me about that one," I said, pointing at the second boat at the dock.

"Yeah, you can rent that. How long?"

"I dunno … maybe a few days," I said, realizing I hadn't given much thought to what I wanted to do.

"Six fifty for four days, eight ninety-five for seven. Gas is extra." She didn't use a lot of unnecessary words.

"OK … let's talk," I said, moving toward her.

She stood her ground, surveying me. "Ever been on one of these before?"

"Nope. But I do have some boat experience. Sail and power."

"OK, these are easy enough. Let's go to the office and wait for Chuck," she said, turning to lead me back to the front of the building.

"How many people?" she asked.

"Just me."

She turned and looked at me with a large question mark as an expression. "No shit?"

"No shit, just me," I grinned.

"You're not runnin' grass or anything stupid like that are you?" She was frowning and the question was serious.

"Nope. No funny business. Just getting away from things for a few days. Actually, for a few months," I said with a nod.

We stopped as she unlocked the door to the office and led me in. She walked behind the counter and pulled out a large pad. It looked like a contract form. She lifted a credit card machine from below and plunked it down on the counter. All the while she had gone back to inspecting me. She was clearly suspicious. I guess single rentals weren't that common.

"So … what are you running from?" she asked out of the blue.

I was a bit startled. She was bold, and yet there was no hint of smart-ass. She was being careful with her curiosity. She genuinely did want to know, I thought.

"A bad marriage," I finally admitted.

"Oh, uhhhh … sorry I asked," she looked away.

"No problem."

"How long?" she asked after a long silence, looking me right in the eyes.

"Ten years."

"Oh … that sucks. That's a pain." She was sincere. She was unhappy that she had probed and touched a sore point.

"Now and then," I confessed. I sat down in the only available chair and waited for the arrival of Chuck, whoever he might be. I decided two could play in this quiz.

"Where are you from?"

"Somewhere else," she said after a brief pause.

"What are you running from?" I pressed.

She looked at me, deciding whether or not to answer my question. At some point, she made up her mind.

"A collection of assholes," she said with a straight face.

"The world's full of them."

"Yeah. My old man being the president of the club."

"You're from the east, aren't you?" It wasn't actually a question. Her slight accent was the giveaway.

"Not any more. Nothin' there for me, and I hate winter," she said succinctly.

"Can't blame you."

The door swung open and a fifty-something man with a full beard entered, nodding to me and smiling at the girl.

"This fella wants to rent 224, Chuck."

"OK … you got some I.D., mister?" he asked, turning to me.

I pulled out my wallet and showed him my driver's license. He nodded.

"How long, Mr. Stephenson?" he asked.

"Four days ... to start with. Maybe seven if it's interesting," I said.

"OK ... we can do that. The season doesn't start for another two weeks, so you get the early rate. Did Pattie tell you about that?"

"Yes. Six-fifty for four days and eight ninety-five for seven, plus gas," I parroted.

"Yep. Credit card?"

I handed him my Visa and he ran it through. Within fifteen minutes I was back on the dock with Chuck and the girl and he was going over the controls, as well as the mechanics of the kitchen, toilet, shower and bunks. It was all pretty straightforward, so I just needed to know where the anchor was stowed, the gas and water tanks located, and I would be set.

"Somewhere I can leave my car?" I asked.

"In back here," he answered. "No one will bother it."

I spent the next few minutes collecting the keys, and moving my stuff from the Outback to the houseboat.

"Where you plannin' on goin'?" Chuck asked.

"I'll just cruise the lakeshore and see what's what. Drop anchor when and where I like and chill out," I volunteered.

He nodded. I didn't need to explain anything more.

"You know where the grocery store is? I need some stuff," I said, looking at them both.

"Askew's is up the road a quarter-mile," Pattie volunteered, pointing.

"Great. I'll take her out for a shakedown and then come back for supplies."

An hour later I was satisfied the boat was in good condition and the controls were serviceable. I had checked the lighting system, the fuel and water supply and the little propane fridge and stove for operation. Everything looked okay. The Yamaha outboard started on the first turn, and the steering, throttle, and transmission were free and positive. I was satisfied.

I locked up after Pattie helped me dock and I drove to the local grocery store. It wasn't big, but it had what I needed. I had made a survey of the houseboat supplies and knew what was on board and what wasn't. I made a list on my shakedown cruise, and was in and out of Askew's in short order.

In less than an hour, I had purchased my supplies and stowed them aboard the boat. I was ready to go.

"Do cell phones work on this lake?" I asked Pattie.

"Yeah … at least to Salmon Arm," she said pointing west. "Not so much up north, though."

"OK … thanks. I'll see you in a few days, I guess."

"Hope so. Don't do anything foolish," she grinned.

She cast off the lines and I carefully backed out of the docking area and onto the lake. I waved to the young woman and turned the wheel full starboard and moved off into the lake. I didn't have a specific destination, but there were so many little towns dotted along the various shores of the two big arms of Shuswap Lake that I didn't worry about it. The boat featured a good marine chart of the area and it would guide me into safe anchorages.

I decided on heading west into Salmon Arm to begin with. There were plenty of locations to visit and plenty of mooring opportunities so I wouldn't have to worry about places to stop and relax. I tuned in a local FM station in Salmon Arm, and motored quietly up the south side of the lake. The scenery was spectacular, but I must have been jaded by my time in the Rockies. As beautiful as it was, I was becoming accustomed to it.

The sun wouldn't set until, well, after nine, but fatigue was beginning to overtake me and I decided that an hour of running would be enough. I began to look for a bay or cove to anchor overnight. It didn't take long and after rehearsing my anchor set-and-retrieval procedure from earlier boating experience, I found a likely spot and dropped the hook.

It was quiet. No wind and an almost cloudless sky. A good start I thought. I walked through the cabin and took the cover off the propane barbeque situated on the stern deck. Something easy… steak, baked potato, salad and some red wine.

As I finished the meal, I began to appreciate how tired I was. There was still daylight at almost ten in the evening, but I was beginning to fade fast. The wine had no doubt hastened that along. I stripped off most of my clothes, pulled on a T-shirt and crawled into the main bunk. In seconds, I was asleep.

For the first time in weeks, I had a single dream. The characters were all familiar. My old boss, my ex-wife Jocelyn, my father and mother, Constance, the mature temptress who had initiated my rehabilitation, and Beth Jorgenson, my most recent lover. It was Beth who seemed to be the focal point of the dream. I couldn't make out what was going on, but they were all yelling at me. Encouraging me to do something... but what? Beth was their leader, but for what?

I awoke in the middle of the pitch-black night and carefully shuffled to the small toilet. I emptied my bladder cautiously without turning on the light, and then made my way back to the bunk, only lightly stubbing my toe on a kick-board. I lay on my back, trying to understand what the dream was about. I looked at my sport watch, pushing the light bar. Three fifteen. The sky would begin to lighten in less than two hours. Fuck! I needed the rest. I rolled over and eventually fell into a restless sleep.

I seldom remember my dreams. They are usually vivid, but confused, and I can't often remember the details. Normally, the dreams were multiple, and my limited awareness of them the next morning was a jumble, mostly a mishmash of all of them without any continuity or reason. When I awoke that morning, I could remember the first dream. I remembered all the people in it and I remembered Beth most of all. Freud would have had fun with this.

I dragged myself out of bed and headed for the shower. I had thought of a quick swim in the lake, but one test of the water temperature with my hand told me my heart wasn't strong enough to withstand the shock of the cold water. I opted for the tiny shower enclosure instead.

By nine o'clock, I had pretty much recovered from my restless night, and fortified with a couple of cups of coffee I was ready to resume my cruise. I toasted a bagel and gulped down a glass of orange juice, topping the whole thing off with a banana. I was fairly certain I would make it until noon.

Sometime after ten-thirty, I spotted a semi-submerged log just ahead and made a quick turn to starboard to avoid it. As I spun the wheel, I heard a bang and suddenly the steering was frozen. Try as I might, I could only move the wheel an inch or two. I killed the engine. I was a couple hundred yards from shore, so I wasn't in any immediate danger, but I needed to find out what the problem was pronto.

I walked back to the engine bay and checked the cable connections to the yoke on the motor. Nothing looked out of place, but there was no moving the cables and the engine was cocked at a thirty degree angle. The only place I was going around in circles unless I could free up the steering.

I reckoned the cables were either underneath the floor or along the side of the platform. I began to look for access panels. I started in the front of the wheelhouse, intending to work backward in the motor systematically. I didn't need to. I found a hatch beneath the pilot's chair on the lower deck and opened it. I used my flashlight to survey what I could see and it only took a couple of minutes to determine the problem.

A die-cast pulley had broken and the cable it guided had slipped down to the inside of the mounting bracket, pinching itself between the hub of the broken pulley and the bracket. Naturally, the pulley was just out of my reach, but at least I knew where the problem was. I withdrew from the hatch and stood up, cursing loudly for anyone to hear.

I gave it some thought and then began a search of the boat to see what I could use as a tool to free up the cable and get the steering centered. As I walked around the upper deck, I noticed a long boat-hook clipped to the roof, and having a close look at it, I noticed it was a two-piece construction. Two screws held the aluminum shaft together and I set about looking for a Phillips-head screwdriver. No such luck!

I searched the kitchen utensils and found a stout knife that might just be strong enough to move the screws if they weren't corroded into place. I didn't hold out much hope, but I had to try.

Some days, the gods are with you, some days they aren't. Today was a good day. I carefully inserted the knife into the screw head, and holding the shaft steady, I began to apply counterclockwise pressure on the screw. Wonder of wonders, it moved. Fifteen sweaty minutes later the two screws were out. I separated the eight-foot boat-hook and at last had a useable length of bar that I could fit into the small hatchway.

I had no way to reduce the tension on the cables, which made my task much more difficult. It took a half-hour to pry the cable loose from its trapped position and snap it over the broken pulley. I was soaked in sweat and in a foul mood. This wasn't the cruise I had in mind.

I pulled myself out of the hatch and immediately went to the little fridge for a beer. Wiping my face and neck with a towel, I took a time-out to regain my composure and decided what will come next. By the time I'd inhaled the beer, I was thinking a little more clearly. I walked back to the motor. This time, I was able to center it, but testing the steering in the wheelhouse, I had very little control over which direction the motor would be aimed.

I was at least three or four hours from the Sicamous dock I had started from yesterday, and it was nearing noon. I had to get myself back there somehow, so I took the only option I could think of. I would steer the motor by using the yoke. I wouldn't have a lot of left-right slack, but at least I could keep it straight, and by disconnecting the linkages to the shifter and power, I could control forward, reverse, neutral, and throttle.

I flipped open my cell phone and dialed the number on the dashboard noted under "In Case of Emergency." Someone actually answered and it was Pattie.

"Pattie, it's me, Lee Stephenson," I announced.

"Oh. Hi Lee. How's the cruise?" she asked cheerily.

"Not so hot," I said with a snarl.

"What's the problem?"

"I have a steering problem and I'm going to have to bring the boat back using my hands on the motor. There's a broken pulley and I'm going to need help docking when I get back." I was beginning to lighten up. Pattie wasn't the cause of this problem.

"Yeah, sure, I can do that. I'll get Chuck and you can tell him what the problem is. When do you figure you'll be back?" she asked, still sounding concerned.

"I dunno… maybe four or five o'clock. I'll call on the cell when I get close."

"Okay… I'll be here. If you run into trouble, call me. I'll bring a boat out to get you," she said.

"Thanks, Pattie. I think I'll be OK, but I'll call and let you know if anything else goes haywire."

I quickly explained what had happened to Chuck and then got ready to move. I turned up the FM radio station to provide some music and entertainment while I began the long slow trip back to Sicamous.

This was not what I had in mind for the next four days. I was pissed and I didn't mind sharing my bad mood.

I got back to Sicamous, just after four. I was tired and my shoulders were aching from keeping the houseboat on a reasonably straight course. The big problem was visibility. I had to keep standing up to make sure I was on the heading I wanted and then twisting to watch my wake to see that it was straight as well. When I could at last see the dock, I was beat -- grateful that this little adventure would be over within a few minutes.

I phoned the office and once again Pattie answered.

"I can see you, Lee. I'm going to come out in the runabout and I'll guide you in. Just sit tight and wait for me, okay?" Pattie was giving me a sense of confidence. She was surprisingly calm and organized for a young, inexperienced woman.

I slipped the motor into idle and then into neutral and drifted toward the dock. Within a minute, I saw the powerboat leave the dock and head directly toward me. She had clearly been prepared for my arrival.

When she got alongside, she threw me a line and I grabbed it in midair.

"Drop the bumpers over this side so I can bring you in a little closer," she said as she came alongside. "I'm going to herd you from here and we'll pull in at the end of the dock to make it easier." She had thought this all out. I smiled at her cool handling of the situation. This girl was more than she appeared.

"Got it," I acknowledged. "I'll slip it into forward but leave it in idle when we're close, okay?"

"Yup!" She eased the runabout into the bumpers on the port side of the houseboat and began to force the bulky craft to crab sideways. She had the technique down pat. I slipped the Yamaha into neutral as we got within twenty feet of the dock and let her push me the last bit. We scuffed the side of the dock gently and I jumped off and quickly secured a line from the bow to the big cleat on the dock. I tied off the stern and breathed a sigh of relief. I was back.

"Nicely done, Pattie," I said with a big, tired smile.

"Thanks." She returned the smile shyly. "Chuck went up to the boatyard to get a new pulley. He'll get it fixed for you by morning.

Sorry about the problem, Lee." I knew she meant what she said. I was too stiff and sore to debate about what the compensation should be, but I thought all things considered, it was just bad luck.

"Nothing to worry about, Pattie. No one got hurt. I'm tired from manhandling the boat, so I'm going to have a shower and then a nap. I'll talk to Chuck in a few minutes."

"Yeah… sure," she said, squinting into the sun as she looked me over. "If you're looking for a good place to eat, try Modine's. Pub food, but good."

"Thanks. What's the nightlife like around here?" I asked.

She laughed. "Nightlife? Well, there's the Pirate's Cove Inn, and the kids usually hang out at Pinocchio's. It's Tuesday, so I don't think 'The Cove' will be very busy, but you never know. I'm headin' over there later. Maybe I'll see you," she grinned.

"Maybe. We'll see," I said noncommittally. "Thanks again for your help. You did a great job guiding me in." I meant it. She handled herself very well for a young woman in a new job. "Where did you learn that?"

"You'd be surprised at how often we have to go rescue someone. Usually just stupid stuff, but in your case, it was trickier. Anyway, I learned in a hurry," she grinned again.

"I can see that. Just the same… well done. I'm impressed," I said.

"Thanks. See you later, maybe."

I smiled as I walked up to the office to see Chuck. It took very little time for me to explain what had happened and Chuck, guessing the problem, had already obtained a replacement pulley and bracket from the plant on the north end of town. I walked back to the boat with him and showed him where the broken part was located and he nodded.

"It'll be tomorrow morning before I can get this done. I've got to take up the deck to get at it. I can give you another craft or I can give you the extra three days at no charge. Will that be OK?"

"Yeah… the extra days… that's more than fair. Can I sleep on the boat tonight?"

"Sure. I won't bother you too early tomorrow morning," he chuckled.

"OK then, I'll take the extra days. That means I don't have to move my stuff and start all over again." I was right, it was more than fair. I wondered what would have happened if it had broken down during the peak season and all their equipment was booked.

Chuck provided a power cord to the boat while I was at the dock and I was set for the night. I wasn't in the mood to cook, and I needed a shower and a change after the exertion of getting the boat moving and back to the dock. I set about rectifying that.

By six that afternoon, I was showered, shaved and changed, feeling much better than I had two hours earlier. I decided to stroll around town and find someplace for supper and then determine what I'd do for the rest of the evening. I didn't want to spend it on a boat, tied to a dock.

I was lucky immediately. I found what looked like a fairly new pub right on the lakefront just three blocks from the boat and checked out the menu at the front door. It looked OK, so I stepped inside to scope it out and I was pleasantly surprised at the surroundings. Large picture windows framed a beautiful view of the lake and mountains to the north. The décor was indeterminate-modern. A postage stamp-sized dance floor was pushed against a small stage at one end of the big room. A live band was advertised for later.

This would do just fine. I looked at the menu cover and it was titled "Modine's."

In the past two months, I had covered a good portion of eastern British Columbia, particularly the Rocky Mountain trench and north. My unbelievable luck in finding willing women had ultimately proven to be just that; unbelievable. Since Beth had left to go back to her home in Vancouver in early April, I was wandering aimlessly. At first, it didn't bother me. I was expecting my incredible streak to end. I assumed it was just a matter of timing and circumstances, and it would all correct itself in time.

By the third week, I had still not made a connection with any woman, and in fact, I hadn't even had very many opportunities. I began to laugh at myself for my arrogance. Was I expecting them to fall into my arms? After all, isn't that what had happened in the first two weeks? Staying at B & B's wasn't conducive to bringing lady-friends back to my room, so I was automatically handicapping myself.

On the other hand, I began to re-examine myself again. I had lived a sheltered life for the most part. Jocelyn, my ex-wife, was actually the only woman I had been with over any length of time. The longest, before or after her was Beth, and that was less than a week. I could hardly consider myself experienced. Nonetheless, the changes to me in the past three months were significant.

I was, I thought, confident in myself, perhaps for the first time. I wasn't worried about where my next meal or next job or even my next bedmate would come from. I was a bit self-absorbed, I admit. Conceit born of success, although short-lived to be sure. I assumed the next woman that was genuinely available would naturally fall to me as surely as the sun would rise in the east. Now that's conceit!

My thoughts and dreams frequently slipped back to memories of Beth. She had produced a more profound effect on me than I was originally willing to admit. She was a powerful, talented, voluptuous woman that any man would lust after. Many already had. What gave me the idea that she would commit herself to someone as non-descript as me? Fantasizing? Probably.

For the past while, my life had become a blur, recent events further confusing my already disoriented psyche. I had no doubt that the effect of the women had been positive. I was also in no doubt that I would seek out someone with whom I would spend my next years. If I was lucky, perhaps for long enough to restore my faith in marriage.

But then again, should I even bother with marriage? My first attempt had ended in failure after ten years. There was no cataclysmic event or sudden, startling revelation. It died slowly and surely, as if stricken by a cancer of the soul. We parted friends, but I was demoralized by having dedicated ten important years of my life to a lost cause. This trip was the beginning of what I hoped was my new life. So far, so good! I was feeling more positive about my future.

As my thoughts returned to the present, I was staring into the bottom of my beer stein. I don't know how long I had been sitting on the bar stool, lost in my reverie. At last, I became aware of the young bartender speaking.

"Another dark ale, sir?" he asked politely.

I shook my head and looked up at him. He had a disarming smile and his eyes sparkled. He liked his job and he was being patient with me.

"Uhhhmmm, yeah, please... and a menu?"

He reached for a thick book on top of a pile of others at the end of the bar and passed it to me.

"The specials are on the blackboard," he said, pointing behind him. "If you have any questions, just ask," he smiled again.

"Thanks." I looked around the pub and noticed there weren't very many people seated. It was just past six thirty, and as Pattie had said, there wasn't much going on Tuesdays. I didn't mind. The TV on the wall behind the bar had a baseball game. Hockey had only just finished with the Stanley Cup. I didn't mind watching the ballgame. You didn't have to pay close attention. It has been just a pastime.

I must have been looking at the menu for several minutes before realizing I hadn't remembered anything I had seen. I snapped it closed and looked up to the blackboard at the specials. Item two was a pulled-pork sandwich with fries and salad. I hadn't enjoyed that southern treat in a long time. I didn't need the menu any more.

My second ale arrived and I ordered the sandwich, relaxing to watch the ballgame until my meal arrived. I was vaguely aware of someone climbing onto the barstool beside me, but I didn't turn my head to look. It was the scent that alerted me.

"You took my advice," her soft voice said. She had leaned into me and spoken into my ear. It was almost a whisper, but not quite.

"What can I get you, Pattie?" The young bartender had appeared from nowhere directly in front of the woman.

"Usual, Barry, thanks," she said, turning back to me.

"Yeah, I did, but more by accident to tell the truth," I replied.

She had changed her clothes and had become a different woman. A white blouse with embroidered patterns at the shoulders, a denim skirt of very short length and a pair of slip-on shoes. Her hair, previously in a tight bun at the back of her neck, was loose and falling about her shoulders. It was black and shone in the bar's halogen spotlights. She looked very sexy and I was immediately interested.

"You look very nice, Pattie," I complimented her.

"Thanks, you clean up pretty good yourself," she smiled. She had a great smile. Nice white, even teeth and lovely brown eyes. Flawless complexion and minimal makeup. A perfect combination.

Barry the bartender appeared with a dark red drink in a tall glass, almost completely filled with ice.

"What's that?" I asked.

"Campari and soda. Barry talked me into trying one a while ago and I liked it," she admitted.

Barry was hovering near the two of us, causing me to wonder if he had designs on Pattie. No need to get him upset, I thought. When at last he wandered off to the far end of the bar, I had my opportunity.

"Barry acts like he has a thing for you," I suggested.

"He does, but it isn't mutual," she answered quickly.

"Does he know that?"

"Yup. So does his very pregnant wife," she said with a bit more emphasis.

"Oh. Good … I mean … good he knows the score," I stammered.

Pattie turned to look at me with a crooked smile.

"Bullshit," she almost whispered again. "You just want to know how many obstacles are in the way between you and me." She spoke with such conviction that I could only nod my agreement. Was I that transparent? Apparently so.

"You've been giving me the 'eye' since we met on the dock yesterday. I know that look. The hungry-man look. You've been going without… maybe since the divorce and now you're getting interested again. I can tell. It doesn't bother me."

She had been speaking in such a low voice that I was sure neither Barry nor anyone else nearby could have overheard the conversation. I wasn't about to confess my activities of the recent past while she was clearing the path for us.

"Have you had supper yet?" I asked.

"Nope. That's why I'm here. Pulled pork night," she said matter-of-factly.

"Funny you should mention that. I just ordered mine. Why don't we make it two … my treat."

"Are you trying to get into my pants?" she asked with a wrinkled brow.

I looked at her for what felt like a long time. "Yes… yes I am," I admitted.

"Well… I've always been a sucker for an honest man," she grinned. "That doesn't mean you'll succeed, Mister."

"Yeah, but… no surprises, no bullshit, and no hidden agenda."

She nodded and signaled for Barry, ordering "the usual" and knowing it would be the pork. She asked him to bring them together and he nodded, looking a bit disappointed.

"So, what do you do for a living, Lee?" she asked as the meals arrived.

"I was an insurance investigator. I checked out claims and made sure they were legitimate. Not all of them, of course. Just the big ones or the ones that looked fishy."

"That would be interesting. You said 'was.' Did you quit?" No beating around the bush with this girl.

"Yeah. It went hand-in-hand with the divorce. I needed a break and some time to decide what came next in my life. I have a job waiting for me in Vancouver with a private detective agency if and when I want it." I was once again surprised how easily I was able to talk about my current life.

"Wow. A private eye, huh?" she said in surprise.

"Yeah … but no guns and no car chases and no dames on the side. Just good old-fashioned grunt work. Not quite as glamorous as the movies and TV make it out to be." I don't think she believed me.

"Just the same… a private eye. I've never met one before."

"You still haven't. I'm not there yet. Still have to go through training and licensing. Nothing's guaranteed," I said.

"Do they teach you how to fight?" she asked, clearly fascinated at my future profession.

"Self defense… that's it. We spend more time on how to legally gather evidence that will hold up in court and how to follow people without being noticed. That's about as glamorous as it gets."

"Do you need a 'Girl Friday'?" She looked hopeful.

"I don't know. I'm not there yet, remember," I laughed. "You want to apply?"

"Damn right! What do I have to do?" she said, fully concentrating on our conversation.

"I haven't a clue. I can give you the name of the company and the people you can talk to about it, but not much more."

"Yes, please!" she jumped.

I pulled one of Pete Dennison's cards out of my wallet and passed it to her.

She looked at it and her eyes grew bigger. "Is this guy a friend?" she asked.

"Yeah. We worked together in some industrial fraud cases when he was a city cop and later when he went to Orca. You'd like him, but I have to warn you, he doesn't look anything like a private investigator. His nickname is 'High School' because of his youthful appearance. Just don't let it fool you. He's very good at his job."

I watched her face as she continued to stare at the business card. She was entranced by the concept. She had little hope of becoming an investigator, but I wasn't about to fire-hose her dream. Barry appeared again with our meals.

We ate in silence for the next few minutes. It wasn't the best pulled pork sandwich I'd ever had, but it was pretty good. The hands-down best went to a little restaurant south of the D. C. -Virginia line called "The Dixie Pig." Just the same, I hadn't had one in a long time and I was enjoying it.

"So Pattie, I don't know your last name," I said, hoping to begin another conversation.

"Monahan," she replied after she'd swallowed a mouthful of sandwich. "Old Toronto Irish."

"And Pattie is short for Patricia?"

"Yup. My old man wanted a boy. It would have been Patrick. Too bad for him and too bad for me. I don't think he ever accepted my coming out a girl," she said with a touch of derision.

"I take it that you and your father are estranged," I suggested.

"That's the polite word for it," she spat, turning to look at me. I had stepped across some line I shouldn't have.

"I'm sorry, Pattie... I know... it's none of my business."

Her face softened and a small smile replaced the flash of anger. "It's OK. You can't help it. You're a detective, remember," she said lightly.

I snorted my reply and went back to finishing my salad. We ate in silence for a couple of minutes.

"He was a classic Irish drunk," she said out of nowhere. "He killed my mother and then he tried to replace her with me. I got out before anything ugly happened, but I won't forgive or forget."

"I'm sorry... I shouldn't have been so nosey." I felt like shit. She was a nice young woman and clearly suffering from a bad parental situation. I'd seen plenty of them before. Alcohol, abuse, abandonment, the whole spectrum of destructive behavior. The innocent victims were just that -- innocent.

"Let's find something more pleasant to talk about," she suggested.

"I'm for that. How long have you been in Sicamous?"

"A year. I got here late May last year and found this job when the guy who was supposed to work with Chuck didn't show up. He was a drunk too, and according Chuck, very unreliable. Chuck had hired him years ago and felt loyal to him, but being a no-show was a no-no, so he hired me when I showed him I could do the job."

"And you plan to head for the coast this fall?"

"Yeah... I suppose. I would like to stop in and see those people at Orca Investigations. I might have something to offer them," she said vaguely. I wondered idly what she meant.

"How do you like this job?" I asked.

"Fine. It gives me lots of time to study, and I can work here at Moline's when the 'seasonals' all go home for the winter."

"What are you studying?"

"Accounting and business management. Distance learning at Ryerson. I get everything online."

"Good for you. How close to your degree?"

"I already have it. This is just some extras I wanted," she said, again with that matter-of-fact tone.

"So... what do you want to do when you're finished the extras?" I asked, genuinely curious.

"I told you. I want something like what you're going to do. I'd love to investigate things… you know… go looking for the facts, the truth. I've been taking forensic accounting at BCIT. Tracking down the crooks with numbers," she laughed.

"Hey… I didn't know you had so much education. Maybe there *is* something Pete or his boss can find for you."

"We'll see. I hope so. I want to do something interesting with my education. I've been on hold for too many years. I need to get on with my life," she said seriously.

I laughed. "You're way too young to be worrying about that yet."

She looked at me with a frown. "How old do you think I am?" she asked sternly.

"Oh shit, not that game again. You know there is no good answer to that question."

"Come on, Mr. Hotshot Detective. How old?"

I slapped my hand over my mouth and groaned. I knew she wouldn't relent until I pushed out a number. Too big and she'd be pissed off, too small and she'd think I didn't take her seriously. "Twenty-five," I surrendered.

"Twenty-eight," she said, still with the sober, serious visage.

"No shit?" I said, surprised.

"No shit."

"Lucky lady. You're going to look great when you're…" I stopped myself. I was about to pull the pin on a grenade. Dumbass, I remonstrated myself. When in a hole, stop digging!

She laughed. The moment of tension was broken and we were back on good terms. No permanent damage.

"So now I know you're no green kid and you have a college education and you have ambition. Now for the tough questions," I smiled. "Can you dance?"

The band had started up and I was much more energized than an hour ago. I'd quit the introspection in favor of being with an attractive woman. Time for seduction mode, I decided.

She didn't answer, but she matched my grin with hers and slid off the stool, holding her hand out to me. I joined her and we walked to the dance floor. We were the only couple at that point, but I didn't care. I just wanted to watch her move.

She was intent on giving a performance for me. She slinked and slithered and slipped around me as she moved to the beat of the three piece group. I recognized the tune, but couldn't name it. I was too interested in staying with Pattie as she made sure I understood her message. I think everyone in the room got the message.

The band had started with a couple of upbeat numbers, but then shifted down into a nice slow, romantic piece and we moved into each other. I felt my arousal growing and I expected she could as well, but I didn't try to hide it and she didn't react to it. I could smell the aroma of her shampoo, mixed with her natural scent. Intoxicating, stimulating, yet subtle, and very sexy.

We held each other closely and we were hardly moving as we swayed to the music. Several other couples had joined us on the small floor and thus we were less conspicuous. When the band took a break several songs later, we moved ourselves to a table and ordered another round.

We continued talking, but I couldn't remember much of it. I was entranced by this dark, intriguing woman. She was confident and yet vulnerable. I wondered about her teenage years and how she got from there to here and collected a degree in the process. It had taken a few years longer than normal, but what obstacles had she overcome? Her comment about her father would have been a key to that answer.

Sometime after ten, two big, rough-looking fellows came into the pub and sat at a table near us. It appeared they had already taken on a fair amount of liquor, but they were looking for more. They looked like construction workers who hadn't bothered to change from their work clothes before coming into the pub.

Barry the bartender had gone off shift an hour or so after we ate and the new guy looked older and a little less in the mood for fun. I saw him say something to the waitress before she came over to see the two new customers and she nodded her head.

When she approached the table, I could tell she was looking them over carefully, trying to decide if she would serve them. She must have chosen to go ahead because she appeared to ask them what they wanted and they told her. She walked back to the bar, stopping for a moment to say something to the bartender.

I stopped paying attention to them when the band returned and I got up and asked Pattie to dance. She smiled and was up immediately, following me to the dance floor. We stayed out there for another four of five songs before the call of nature began to impose itself on me. I took Pattie back to our table and excused myself, heading for the washroom. Three pints of beer tend to do that.

When I made my way back to our table, the two big guys were standing there, leaning over Pattie. She didn't look happy. I was pretty sure she didn't invite them, so I walked over and interrupted.

"Excuse me, gentlemen. Is there something I can help you with?" I asked politely.

"Fuck no. We were asking this lady if she wanted to join us at our table. We figured she'd be much happier sitting with real men instead of a wimp like you," he sneered. I could smell the alcohol on his breath from several feet away. I'm sure it must have almost overpowered Pattie since their faces had been inches from hers.

"Well, what does the lady have to say about that?" I asked, barely able to maintain a civil tone.

"Who gives a fuck. She'll come when she's told to." He was having trouble standing without weaving.

I turned to the bartender to get his attention. I didn't need to. He nodded and I could see him reach for the phone under the bar.

"Tell you what guys. You really don't want any trouble with the police, and forcing this young lady to do something she doesn't want to do could be a very, very big mistake." I couldn't make my warning any more clear.

"Fuck off, pussy," was the slurred reply.

"No... you fuck off, asshole," Pattie snapped. "The last thing I want is to have anything to do with you two drunken clowns." She wasn't happy with them.

They looked down at her, bleary-eyed and weaving.

"Come on, you're coming with us. We're gonna' have some fun," the larger one said, reaching for Pattie's arm.

I wasn't sure if or when the cops were going to arrive, but I knew I couldn't let them man-handle Pattie. I also wasn't sure if I could get any help from the bartender, but I had to do something now. I reached out and grabbed the shirt collar of the smaller guy, yanking him back toward me and kicking his legs out from under him. He went down like a sack of cement.

I turned to the bigger guy and moved around the table behind Pattie. I put one hand on her left shoulder and the other on the back of her chair. I gave her one clear instruction.

"When I say 'go,' go!" I wasn't watching her and I had no idea if she acknowledged me or not. The big guy was still weaving, trying to figure out what I was up to while the smaller guy was trying to pick himself up off the floor but not having much success.

"Go!" I shouted as I yanked Pattie's chair back. She moved like a cat and ran towards the bar. The big guy turned as if to follow her and as he did, I shoved the table as hard as I could. The sharp corner of the tabletop hit him in the hip, and then his crotch, and he went down howling in pain.

I was about to consider making for the exit with Pattie, when both the bartender and the local RCMP showed up. The barkeep had what looked to be nightstick in his hand and was clearly contemplating using it on the skull of the first guy to cause any more trouble. The RCMP constables put an end to that.

We hung around for a few minutes while one of the constables took our statements. The two louts were cuffed and taken off to the local holding cell for the night. Drunk and disorderly would likely be the charges. Pattie and I looked at each other and began to laugh. I guess it was a release of tension, but it was all so stupidly bizarre and comedic. We decided that was enough for now.

"You're a fun date, you know," I laughed as we walked outside into the cool night air.

Pattie chuckled, "I didn't know it was a date. If it was, it was the craziest I've had. Those two idiots kind of scared me though. They were just drunk enough to do something very stupid," she added seriously.

"Yes, I think you're right. They had me worried too. They looked like a couple of tough characters. I wouldn't have wanted to deal with them sober," I admitted.

"It didn't stop you," she said, looking at me with her lovely smile. "You did what you had to and kept things from getting out of hand. The damsel in distress has been saved."

"We've kind of had our evening messed up. I wanted to dance with you some more."

"You just wanted me close, holding me... right?" she challenged as she moved toward me.

"Yes... that's exactly what I wanted." I wrapped my arms around her, kissing her as she sagged into my body. The nervous energy of the last few minutes was slowly dissolving and I felt the passion building. She must have sensed it too.

"Why don't we go down to the boat? No one will bother us there," she said softly.

I took her hand, wrapping my other arm around her shoulder, and pulled her to my side as we walked slowly down the street toward the dock. We didn't talk, but a lot of information was being exchanged over those three blocks. Whether it was the fear, adrenalin, alcohol, or something else, we were about to change our relationship.

I unlocked the door of the houseboat and flicked on the lights. Pattie pulled the curtains and I dimmed most of the lights to give us some sense of atmosphere.

"Would you like something?" I asked.

"Yes... you," she said without hesitation.

"I think I have lots of that," I smiled, reaching for her.

We were undressed in seconds and quickly in the already made-up double bed. Pattie appeared to be tense from our previous adventure, so I tried to slow the pace and involve her in foreplay. She was having none of it.

"Don't make me wait... please, Lee," she implored. I could tell by the tone of her voice that she wasn't going to be patient.

I stroked the tip of my now-leaking cock along her slit to provide some lubrication. It took only seconds to determine that she was ready, willing and able to have me enter her. So I did, slowly at first, and then progressively deeper with each measured stroke. She was arching her back as I moved into her. She tried to take even more of me. It wasn't long before I was fully enveloped in her hot, tight center.

I stopped for a moment to give her a chance to settle, but she didn't appear to need or want that. She slapped my ass as she grabbed a handful of gluteus maximus, pulling me urgently into her even further, all the while thrusting her hips upward in a determined bid to spear herself on my cock.

It was frantic and fantastic, electric and uncontrolled. All the fear and tension of the earlier confrontation exploded into her wild, tormented gyrations. I hung on as best I could, but it couldn't last forever. I was about to warn her of my coming when she roared her release, her back forming a rigid arc from her head to her heels, suspending me on this bridge of flesh. She must have held me there for several seconds before she collapsed with me crashing down upon her, unable to protect her. I heard a loud "ooohmmph" as I landed. I prayed I hadn't hurt her.

"You okay?" I gasped.

"Oh shit... what happened?" she moaned.

"Did I hurt you? I landed right on you."

"You did? I didn't notice, I guess." She was panting and slowly regaining her senses.

"That was amazing. Now I know what 'awesome' really means," she laughed softly between gasps.

"You were pretty charged up. The adrenalin and everything, I guess."

"Hey... I can feel you. You're still there. Didn't you come yet?" she asked as her hand probed my still-rigid member.

"No problem. It won't go bad," I chuckled.

"Oh... that means I can have another, doesn't it?" she grinned, and she rolled her leg over me.

"I guess it does, but how about you on top and that way I can't fall on you again." It didn't seem like I'd hurt her ... or that she'd even been aware of our collision.

"I don't know. If you can make me come like you just did, you can fall on me any time you like."

"I think that was mostly you. I was just the stick stirring the pot."

"Yeah, but what a nice stick."

She rose on all fours and then slithered down my body until she reached my manhood. She took it in her hand and examined it for a moment and then lowered her head and took me in her mouth. For the next five minutes, she treated me to the most loving, careful, oral sex I had ever experienced. I was hard again and once more I had to warn her.

"I'm close, Pattie. Do what you want to do. Don't worry about me." My voice cracked with the tension.

She continued to lick and suck and tease and stroke for a few seconds before rising up and mounting me, aiming my rigid cock into her very wet, hot pussy. I didn't expect to last a single stroke, but I was wrong. It wasn't long, but at least it wasn't immediate. I let go after warning her again and she maintained her position, her eyes watching mine, a smile on her face. She was enjoying herself a great deal and I enjoyed providing her fulfillment.

We managed a third time after I had applied my oral skills to her and she to me once more. We couldn't duplicate the explosive orgasm she experienced in the beginning, but it didn't matter. We were both happy and satisfied.

"Can you stay?" I asked hopefully.

"Hmmm, that would be nice," she murmured.

"I'll make breakfast. What time do you have to start work?"

"I don't. I get the next two days off," she said, lifting her head to look at me.

"Well then, what about spending them with me?"

"Love to." There wasn't any doubt in her answer.

"I'll get some Campari at the store tomorrow and we'll be set. I've got lots of supplies for the next few days."

"I need to get some stuff from my place before we go. Girl stuff, you know?"

"Yeah. No rush, we'll just meander up the lake and go wherever we want."

She was lying on my chest, drowsy from her exertions and the excitement of the earlier confrontation.

The next morning, I woke at seven, later than I had been used to in the past month. Pattie was curled up with her back to me, my arm over her hip, and my hand cupping a lovely breast as she slept. I thought back over the previous evening and our decision to spend the next two days together. I was happy about that.

She was a delight to be with, and I wanted to know more about her. I wondered if she would ever tell me... tell anyone... about her past. I made a trip to both the grocery store and the liquor store while Chuck fixed the steering and Pattie went home for clothes and toiletries. She returned just before ten and a few minutes later we cast off.

The next two days were wonderful, and I hated to head back to the dock on Friday to drop Pattie off. We had laughed and loved and talked about everything we could think of. I told her about my marriage and why I ended it. I told her about my first two weeks of debauchery, but not in any detail. I did let her know that I looked at it as therapy and that it had been a benefit to my mental state. She seemed to understand and accept that.

We didn't pretend we would be faithful to each other or that we had a future beyond this encounter, but we did promise to stay in touch, at least by e-mail.

Pattie let me into her past a little, but still held back the gory details and the issues surrounding her relationship with her father.

I was convinced she would be successful at whatever she put her mind to. She had that sense of dedication that wouldn't let anything stop her if it was within her reach. I would happily phone Pete Dennison and tell him about her. I expected they would give her a fair hearing.

When I dropped Pattie off at the dock, it was with disappointment. I knew that the remaining three days were not going to be as pleasurable as the previous two. On top of that, it looked like it might rain.

I was back where I started, alone again. I shouldn't complain, I said to myself. I had two days and three nights with a wonderful young woman and like my other encounters earlier, I wouldn't easily forget her. Some guys never get that much in their entire lives. Call yourself lucky, Lee Stephenson.

When I pulled up to the dock on Sunday afternoon, Pattie was standing there waiting for me. I was delighted. She was exactly the tonic I needed at the finish of my cruise. I jumped off the boat to tie off the forward line to the dock cleat while Pattie handled the stern. In seconds we were in each other's arms. I saw Chuck watching from the office window. I swore he had a smile on his face.

"I'm not going anywhere until tomorrow. I'll get a motel room. Care to join me for dinner and 'afters?'" I blurted out in a stream.

She laughed. I was like a teenager with a crush on the cheerleader and didn't know how to handle himself.

"Yeah, I guess," she smiled, her head cocked and her eyes squinting at me.

I was hoping I'd have another chance to be with her and it looked like I was in luck.

"I can't stay the night, though. I've got an exam tomorrow and I need to be prepared."

"Can you stay for a little while?" I must have sounded like I was begging. I was.

"Sure, for you," she smiled.

"Do we dare try Modine's again?"

She laughed again. "Well, you know what they say about lightning striking twice in the same place."

"Modine's it is then. Six o'clock?"

"Six thirty. Let me go home and get cleaned up first."

"Six thirty. I'll be there." I leaned over and kissed her, my hand brushing her breast, and she responded. I was back on that high she so easily created in me.

"See you then," she smiled, turning to head back to the boat.

I had already packed my stuff and leftover food in the two plastic storage tubs I kept in the car and placed them on a dolly to transport them up to my car. Five minutes later I was in the office with Chuck, signing off on my Visa and getting a receipt.

"No more problems, Mr. Stephenson?"

"Nope… everything went fine. It's very lovely up here. It's my first time on Shuswap."

"A lot more fun if there's someone to share it with," he said with a grin.

"You're absolutely right. I'm going to remember that next time," I smiled. "Thanks, I enjoyed myself."

"You're welcome. Come back anytime," he said, undoubtedly meaning it.

Pattie appeared at my table just past six thirty and once again surprised me. She was wearing a dress. A low-cut, slinky dress. A sexy, low-cut, slinky dress in a shiny black material. It fit her very closely. So closely, I was sure she wasn't wearing a bra and possibly no panties.

"Wow!" I said it and I meant it. She was a knockout and she knew it. I was trying to stand like a gentleman, but I wasn't quick enough for her. She dropped into her seat and her prominent nipples bounced inside the slippery fabric. She looked hot and the promise of the evening was now confirmed. No woman on earth wore a dress like that without expecting hormonal reactions from any male with a pulse.

"I figured you'd like it," she grinned, her eyebrow arching as she gave me another of her knowing, sideways looks.

"I think every guy within a hundred miles likes it." My eyes must have been popping out of my head. She had added some extra makeup around her eyes and the lipstick was a more aggressive deep red. She didn't look like the same woman I had connected with at Modine's on Tuesday. This was a much more forceful statement. I caught a glimpse of her feet and saw she was wearing a pair of black patent-leather high heels. It was the complete look of a woman out for trouble and knowing she'd find it. I fully intended to be that trouble.

"To what do I owe the honor of your attire?" I asked with a grin.

"I just wanted to say thanks. This was a great week. I truly enjoyed being with you. You are someone special to me. You've helped me a lot, Lee."

She was, I felt, sincere. She meant it. She knew exactly how to pump up my ego. Not that it needed much pumping this past few days.

"So tell me... how did I help you?"

"You made me feel good about myself again. I've been waiting for someone. I haven't wanted to be with anyone until you came along. Not lately anyway. I don't know how, but I thought you were different," she said, searching my face.

"I think you're giving me too much credit. I'm not that... noble. You were nice, attractive and available. It was as simple as that," I said, trying not to sound too cold.

"Unh uh... sorry, no sale. You may not think so, but that's not you. You may be trying to figure yourself out, but that's not you," she said with certainty.

I turned away from her and looked at my hands. "Maybe not, but I'm still trying, Pattie. I don't want to hurt you. I don't want you to expect more from me than I can give."

"I don't. I don't want or need more. I like who you are. The sex is perfect, and the time we spend together is too. Don't go overanalyzing it." She was looking at me intently now.

"You're not the first person who's made that comment," I admitted.

"You two must have done a lot of damage to each other."

"You mean Jocelyn?"

"Who else?"

"I never thought of it that way. I just thought it was like... a slow death."

"The most painful death of all, they say."

I looked at her for a few moments. "You're pretty worldly for someone as young...." I paused again.

She grinned. She couldn't help it. "There you go again, underestimating my age."

"Underestimating your savvy, too."

Her eyebrows popped up and she once again used that head-cocked look that had become familiar. The waitress arrived just in the nick of time. I ordered a Campari and soda for Pattie and a dry Australian red for me. I intended to pace myself tonight. I wanted every sensual moment I could have with her to be remembered.

It was. We ate, but I wasn't paying as much attention to the food as I was with Pattie. We danced and it didn't matter whether it was fast or slow, we just wanted to be touching each other, holding each other. We left early and I drove her to my motel room. I had turned the bed down and closed the curtains before I left for the pub. A single lamp in the far corner of the room was all the light I wanted.

I took her in my arms and allowed my hands and fingers to roam over her lovely body. The dress was so smooth and silky and elegant and so easily removed. She helped undress me and we slid beneath the single sheet, turning toward each other.

"This will be the last time, Lee," she said quietly.

"I know. Let's make it special. Ladies choice."

"I've already chosen. I chose you. Now… show me what you want to show me," she said smiling.

We began kissing as I willed myself to take it slowly and linger at each point. Her lips, ears, her neck, shoulders, breasts, navel and at last, her inner thighs. I would take my time, and yet I would listen and be alert for her physical responses. As I began to touch her labial lips with my tongue, my lips and even my teeth, she began to send me more urgent messages. Her hips found a slow, rhythmic pulse and her hands clasped the back of my head. The dance had begun.

I don't think I have ever lasted that long in one sexual encounter in my life. In some way, we were so perfectly in tune with each other that it didn't require any effort. It was as natural as breathing, and yet much more rewarding. There was no hurry for either of us. I watched her watch me and smiled as she smiled. It was exactly what we were seeking for our farewell.

Pattie had intended to go home early to prepare for her next accounting examination, but it didn't work out that way. Neither of us could halt the inevitable, nor did we want to. It was so right and so comfortable and so erotic, that there was no way to bring it to an unnatural end. Ultimately, exhaustion and her inability to produce more natural lubrication announced our completion.

We lay in each others arms for some time before we rose and dressed. I followed her out the door to my car and drove her home. We kissed and held each other again, reluctant to end it, but Pattie broke the embrace, smiled, and slipped out the car door. She turned and leaned into the open window, smiling.

"Goodbye, Leighton. I wish you luck and a safe journey. I think you will find what you are looking for. Thank you again for all you gave me. I won't forget." With that, she turned and entered the door of her apartment. I wondered if I would ever see her again.

Later that morning, I was on my way once more. I had a new career awaiting my word that I was ready to begin. It was, I hoped, an exciting break from my more mundane role as an insurance investigator. Time would tell, but I was optimistic. In the meantime, I wasn't in a rush to go home, but thanks to Pattie, I was feeling much more alive. The time to return home wasn't far off.

Part 6 – Charlie

It felt quite natural to be on the move again. My initial flurry of sexual encounters with women had lasted but a short two weeks before I suffered a two month long dry spell. I was in no danger of falling into depression over it, but I was wondering what had happened to the magic. Pattie Monahan had solved all that.

As I looked in the rear-view mirror of my Outback, I was imagining I could see her standing there, waving goodbye to me. Our little fling had lasted four nights, broken up over a one week period. She was a dynamic, talented, and bright young woman that I could easily have stayed with much longer. It wasn't what she wanted. She had plans.

When I stopped for lunch, I phoned Peter Dennison, my contact at Orca Investigations.

"Hi Pete, how are you?"

"That you, Lee? Good to hear from you. You coming in?" he asked for the hundredth time.

"Naw … not quite ready yet. I'll let you know. Don't go holding anything open on my account. I'm in no rush."

"So, how are you doing? Where are you?"

"Salmon Arm, heading for Kamloops."

"Lots of good looking ladies in Kamloops," he needled.

"Hope so. I just had a nice break in Sicamous with one. She's someone you should talk to, Pete," I said seriously.

"Oh… how come?"

"She's got a degree in Business Admin, and she's taking a course on forensic accounting. I know she wants a job in your field."

"Is her name Pattie Monahan?" Pete asked with a chuckle.

"Yeah… I should have known. She didn't waste any time, did she? I gave her your card. I think you should talk to her."

"Don't worry, we will. We're looking for someone in that field to start as a 'junior.' She sounds like a good candidate. Thanks for thinking of us."

"Well, to tell the truth, I was thinking of me. If I end up working there... well, you get the picture," I said, smiling to myself.

"Yeah, well don't expect me to save her for you. I'm a poor, lonely bachelor too, you know," he laughed.

"I've already warned her about you. Good luck!"

"Hey Lee... seriously... when are you comin' in?"

"Don't know for certain, Pete, but I'm pretty sure I'm not going to be out here on my own for much longer. I think I've gotten over the worst of it and I'm starting to think more about the future than I did when I set out in March. Hell, it's still only June... at least let me enjoy the summer."

"Okay, okay, I get it. No more pressure. Just take care of yourself and stay in touch. Harold and I are still serious, Lee. The job's here if you want it. We mean that."

"Thanks, Pete. I've been hanging on to that thought all along. I just need to make sure that when I do, I've dumped all the baggage, capiche?"

"Yeah, I got it. Take care, Lee."

I was glad to hear they were interested in Pattie. I was confident she had something to offer. She was more mature than most 'juniors,' and was clearly very bright. She was also tough enough to work in a male-dominated environment without being intimidated. It would be interesting to watch her progress if she was hired.

It isn't that far from Sicamous to Kamloops; about eighty miles by road. I was in no rush since I thought I had a place to stay, The Ghost Town Lodge. It was a rustic resort ranch located in a ghost town a few miles north of Kamloops. I had a standing invitation to drop in anytime from the owner, Lew Coulson.

I met Lewis Coulson during my work as an insurance investigator. He had contacted us when fire destroyed his dude ranch in 100 Mile House and we were the insurance carrier. Lew suspected foul play, although the local fire department found no evidence of it. Lew was a straight-up guy and said he would feel better about accepting the settlement check when his doubts were put to bed. He told me that his suspicions were originally aroused when he received several unsolicited offers to buy the property at what he thought were unusually generous numbers.

As it turned out, Lew was right. Someone had torched the building, but it had been done by a pro, and it wasn't surprising the local volunteer fire department had missed the signs. After talking to Lew and trying to figure out a motive, we discovered that there had been a previous land claim under dispute before Lew owned the property. When the original title search had turned up nothing to obstruct his purchase, I began to smell a rat.

Sure enough, the original title records had been hidden or destroyed, and false ones had been substituted. When I matched the phony records with records from the era of the original title, I could see that there was no comparison in the forms. Then it was a matter of finding out who and why.

It took a lot of plain old-fashioned digging, but we finally found a mining claim at the root of the mystery. Apparently, the district clerk knew of the claim, and thinking that he could get the valuable property at a huge discount, prepared the phony documents and hired a "pro" to torch the buildings.

Just one problem. The original claim had been filed with an error. They had specified the adjacent property location and the land noted in the title was virtually worthless. Nonetheless, my company was happy since they could claim against the district for our costs, and Lew was happy because he knew the truth, and came out of it with a nice profit from a legitimate sale.

Over that six-week period, I might have been forced to live in motels weekdays, facing a weekly drive to and from Vancouver to my work. Lew, however, opened his home to me, a fully furnished forty-foot mobile, and we became good friends.

Lew had always wanted to have a "cowboy lodge" as he called it, and when the now-defunct town of Burnt Creek was put up for sale, he jumped at it. Within days, the mobile home had been moved onto the property, and he began restoring the buildings to create his lodge. It took two years to finish, but people came from all over the world to experience the "old west" atmosphere at the *Ghost Town Lodge*.

I phoned Lew from my cell and let him know I was in the vicinity and would like to stop by and visit. As expected, that turned into an invitation to stay with him at the lodge and I happily took him up on it. I arrived just after five that afternoon and was greeted by an enthusiastic Lew with a fine looking woman at his side.

After we had exchanged hearty hellos and finished with our back-slapping, Lew turned to the woman and took her hand.

"Lee, this is my lady, Francine," he said with obvious pride.

"Hi Francine, and congratulations. I was wondering if anyone would ever tie this guy down."

"Hi Lee. Lew's done nothing but talk about you since you called. It's wonderful to meet you," she said with a bright, toothy smile. "Let's get out of this hot sun and go inside."

I hadn't been in the lodge since it was finished and I was struck by how large and wonderfully authentic it appeared. It was a timber frame construction with a huge great room and dining area, and a staircase at each end leading up to several loft rooms. Lew gave me the tour and we ended up in the back of the main floor where he showed me a spare bedroom for my stay. Francine had disappeared into the kitchen to continue with the evening meal preparation.

"We're full, happily," Lew said when I asked about the business. "Have been almost since we opened. We renovated some of the other buildings for more capacity and I think we're going to have to expand the kitchen and the barn. Our guests are all out on a trail ride right now, but they'll be back soon. Why don't you settle in and we can talk after dinner. We've got a lot of catching up to do."

I took the hint, brought my gear in, took a quick shower in the ensuite, and changed my clothes. I was looking forward to some time with Lew and learning about what was going on in his life, especially about Francine. She was a good looking lady and I was happy for my friend.

I had barely returned to the great room when the first of the trail riders arrived, stomping their feet in a hopeless attempt to knock the dust off. I noticed they were mostly my age, in their thirties, with the odd sprinkling of forty and fifty-somethings as well. They all acknowledged my hello with curious glances and then moved upstairs to their rooms, presumably to shower and change.

I wandered back to the kitchen to see if I could help Francine and found Lew there, working side-by-side with her. It looked like they had a system that worked for the two of them, but I thought I could at least contribute delivery to the dining table. I volunteered and my offer was accepted.

Francine explained that she had come to the lodge as a cook when it first opened. The room I was using was hers to begin with. It didn't take long for her and Lew to fall in love, and now both slept in the master quarters at the other end of the main floor. They hadn't gotten around to getting married yet, but I could tell it was on their minds. Lew had never married, but Francine had a failed one behind her, just as I did. I guessed she was in her mid-thirties, so she was a bit younger than Lew, who was two years older than me.

Dinner would be served at seven, and by six o'clock couples were beginning to assemble in the great room for happy hour after they had changed and showered. They were a boisterous and happy lot who got along well with each other.

I volunteered to help at the bar. Lew told me that drinks were on the house, within reason. He asked me to use my best judgement and that was all he said.

Beer and wine looked to be the preferred libation, although an older couple from Germany preferred vodka and lime juice. I nursed a red wine as I watched the couples interact and tried to guess what they must have paid for this two week holiday. As I chatted casually with them, having introduced myself, I learned three couples were from Ontario, two from Quebec, three from the U.S. and two from Europe.

The couple from England was the life of the party and kept everyone around them laughing. I noticed one woman, however, who appeared to be on her own. I couldn't spot a partner and she was drifting from group to group, engaging in light conversation and then moving on. When she came to the bar for another white wine, I introduced myself.

"Hi... I'm Lee Stephenson. I'm a friend of Lew Coulson."

"Nice to meet you Lee. I'm Charlie Kennedy," she replied in a bright voice.

"Charlie? That's an unusual name. Short for... Charlotte?" I guessed.

"I wish. It's short for Charline," she said with a look of disgust.

"Well, Uhhhmmm... that's a very lovely name as well," I stammered.

She laughed… more of a guffaw in fact. "Don't drink much more of that wine, Lee. It's affecting your judgement," she said with a big smile.

"I'll be careful. So… where do you hail from?"

"The Big Smoke… Toronto. I wanted a real western experience and this looked like a good bet."

"And?"

"It's great. I'm back riding for the first time since I was thirteen and I'd forgotten how much I enjoyed it. And this place," she said, her hand waving around the lodge, "is fantastic. Wait 'til you sample the meals."

"Are you joining us for supper?" she asked after a moment's pause.

"Yes… I've been invited to stay as long as I don't embarrass myself."

"Somehow, I don't think that's likely. Now my boy … uh … ex-boyfriend, he majored in embarrassing behavior. It's one of the reasons I'm on my own at this shindig." She had just answered a very important question without my having to ask. Thank you!

She was giving me the impression of a very worldly woman, about forty-five years old I guessed. She was very attractive in her western garb with the tight jeans and brightly colored blouse showing her solidly built figure off to her advantage. This was no "Skinny Minnie," but a well-endowed all-female woman. She also appeared to be plain-spoken, and I figured the ex-boyfriend had trod on her toes somewhere along the line. It would be interesting to know.

Since we were both on our own, we sat together at the dining table and I thoroughly enjoyed both the meal and the company. The English couple was across the table from us and kept everyone laughing with their unfailing good humour. I didn't learn a lot more from Charlie with all the table talk and clatter, but I could do that later. She was a great dinner companion and I was pleased to have the good luck to find her so quickly. It was a reminder that my good fortune with women had returned.

When the meal ended and we moved to the bar for after dinner drinks, I resumed my role as bartender to allow Lew and Francine to clear the dishes and take a break. The dinner had been superb and there wasn't a dissenting voice in the house. I was conscious that Charlie had hung by the bar as I worked to pass out the liqueurs and coffees. I was getting the impression she was a bit lonely and maybe I could provide the company.

As I dispensed the drinks, Charlie and I had a chance for more conversation. The noise and cross-talk of the dinner table were gone and the group had broken up into small clusters, their voices no longer competing with each other. The sumptuous meal had slowed everyone down to a calmer, more satisfied pace.

"I know you're enjoying the riding, Charlie, but are you having a good time here?" I was back to my confident new self.

"Yes," she answered without hesitation. "I like the people and I love the place, and it just confirmed that the asshole I was with was a bad mistake."

"So don't beat around the bush, tell me how you really feel," I laughed.

"God, Lee… he was such a dickhead. I have no idea why I thought I should be with him. I must be losing my grip." She was shaking her head in wonder at the thought.

"Well, in a way I'm sorry to hear that … then again … in a way, I'm not."

She looked at me and smiled. She got the message.

"So what's a good looking guy like you doing on his own?"

"Ah … well … recently divorced and working on my rehabilitation."

"Good for you. That's exactly the right thing to do. I speak from experience."

"Oh … sorry to hear that," I said without looking at her.

"Don't be. I made a mistake and I fixed it. Simple as that. Trouble is, I'm making the same mistake again more often than not." Her voice was tinged with regret.

"You just need a change in luck. You're a lovely woman and smart, and you'll find the right guy one of these days," I assured her.

"Thanks. I needed that," she laughed. "Want to apply for the job?"

I was taken aback by her comment, but recovered. "What makes you think I'd be any different?"

"Oh, I don't know. Just a hunch, I guess. You don't act like some of the 'Desperate Desmonds' that I've been dating. I get the feeling that you are a lot more in control than most guys." Her raised eyebrow and crooked smile left me little doubt she was challenging me.

"Looks can be deceiving," I suggested with a sideways glance.

"Yeah ... I found that out ... for sure. Somehow, I don't think I'm wrong, though." She had turned toward me and I could clearly see a more confident Charlie.

The activity at the bar had tapered off and Lew had turned on some music. It was soft, easy on the ears and a reasonably slow tempo. The lively English couple, the German pair and two or three others began to dance and that gave me my opportunity.

"Would you care to dance?" I asked.

"Love to," she answered quietly.

Often when I dance I have two left feet, but Charlie was so easy to lead and felt so comfortable in my arms that we were soon alone in our own world.

"How long are you here for?" I asked as we danced.

"I just got here Saturday, so today's day three. I'm booked for two weeks. How about you?"

"Not sure. I don't want to overstay my welcome, and I can't offer Lew much help in this business, so it probably won't be too long."

"Well, just remember ... I have booked and paid for a double ... so ... if you're interested, I could find some room for you." Again, her eyes had that mischievous twinkle, challenging me with just a look.

"Hmmm ... very tempting. Let's just see how we get along before we make any big decisions. You've already had one disappointment. You don't need another." I was serious, but also very interested. We seemed to hit it off and a few days with another delightful woman would be quite pleasant.

"You're being cautious ... but I agree. We should know pretty soon if we want to team up," she smiled.

We continued to dance and she was moving right into me, insinuating her body on mine. She had a lot to insinuate with and it felt great. I always did like full-figured women and Charlie was definitely my type. The thought crossed my mind that she might want to take a "test drive" at some point. Ever the optimist, I wondered if tonight might be the night.

"You never did tell me what you did ... I mean ... your career," I said as we moved slowly together.

"You'll laugh. I own a body shop."

"How do you spell that?" I was feeling pretty confident now.

"Careful, Lee. I might take offense."

I didn't take her warning seriously. "So ... what's a nice girl like you doing in a place like that?"

"I inherited it from my father. He got sick and couldn't run it anymore, so I took it over. I've been pretty successful, as a matter of fact."

It sounded to me like it was a point of pride, so I ran with it. "Why am I not surprised? You look like a no-nonsense kind of woman, so you wouldn't be intimidated by the macho-male atmosphere."

She smiled at me but didn't reply. I had made my point and she had no need to confirm it. She wanted to maintain some sense of femininity, I thought. It was completely unnecessary. She was genuinely all-woman. I was very attracted to her and I was confident she knew that.

The trail ride and the various other activities had caught up with many of the guests and gradually they all began to disappear. Charlie and I were sitting on the sofa and exchanging small talk about ourselves when Lew and Francine appeared from the back.

"All done for the day?" I asked Francine.

"Yes ... all ready for tomorrow," she smiled.

"What time do you get up?"

"Six ... breakfast at seven-thirty to eight-thirty. Don't be late," Lew laughed.

"He's right, Lee. The breakfasts are amazing," Charlie chimed in.

"I see you two have met and got acquainted already," Francine grinned.

Charlie turned and looked at me. "I've traded up, as you can see," she smirked.

I don't usually blush, but I'm sure I did then.

"Well, we certainly aren't going to miss your original partner," Lew said seriously.

"Was it that bad?" I asked.

"I was ten seconds away from calling the Mounties when he finally got the message that he wasn't welcome," Lew admitted.

"Wow ... what did he do to cause that?"

It was Charlie who answered my question.

"He almost immediately got drunk, made a pass at a couple of married women, including Francine, and generally made an unpleasant scene. When Lew asked him quietly to behave, he got belligerent and threatened to beat Lew up. I was mortified, and I guess I was yelling at him to stop and ... I don't know. I just lost it I guess."

Lew picked up the story from there.

"I eventually got him calmed down enough and finally he stomped off to their room. I had Charline stay in the room you're in just to make sure he didn't do anything stupid, and on Sunday morning he was missing. His kit and car were gone. Good riddance, we all agreed," he concluded.

"It was all my fault," Charlie confessed. "He didn't want to come on this vacation in the first place. He called it my juvenile fantasy. I was stupid enough to think he'd change his mind when he got here." Her look of regret was clearly defined by her frown and downcast eyes.

"No harm done, Charlie," Francine broke in. "He's gone and you're having the fun you wanted to have when you booked here. Why, we've even arranged for a new dance partner for you," she said with a self-satisfied grin.

Charlie turned back to me and smiled. She had been embarrassed by the actions of her ex-boyfriend, but I sensed she was relieved that it was over. No damage had been done to either the hosts or the guests. Just an unhappy event that was soon forgotten.

"I think I've come out of this ahead," Charlie volunteered as she looked at me. Her gaze was unwavering and her bright blue eyes didn't blink.

I said nothing, but I was pretty sure there was a smile on my face.

We sat there, chatting comfortably as Lew talked about the plans for the lodge and his need to hire some additional help as the place grew.

There were currently ten rooms and that meant twenty meals, three times a day, plus housekeeping and maintenance. They had help in the barn from an old local cowhand who looked after the horses and the trail rides. Lew handled the bookings and there was a part-time bookkeeper for the accounts.

If they expanded to handle up to ten or twenty more couples, they would need more help to manage the extra people and facilities. Their operation was virtually full from April to October, so any expansion would have to happen in the five quiet months. Both Lew and Francine were genuinely enjoying their life. It was demanding but they were well suited to the task.

I volunteered my limited skills for the remainder of my stay, and they happily accepted. Both of them knew the reason for my travels this spring and summer, and sometimes having a task is helpful therapy as well. Charlie noticeably brightened when I made it clear that I would stay as long as I could be useful. I was pretty sure Francine picked up on that as well.

It was ten o'clock when Francine and Lew shuffled off to their quarters. I poured Charlie and I, each a small brandy and returned to my place beside her.

"It sounds like you had an exciting start to your vacation," hoping I wasn't opening an old wound.

"That's an understatement!" She was shaking her head. "I don't know what I was thinking when I invited him. I didn't even like him that much. I guess it was a sign of desperation."

"I find it hard to believe you would be desperate." I meant it. She was a handsome and very alive woman who should immediately attract men.

"I suppose that my business life puts some of them off. I'm at the shop all day, every day but Sunday. We often work nights on special projects."

"You do some of the work yourself?" I asked, surprised.

"Yup. Dad taught me just about everything I needed to know, and he still does. I can handle an English Wheel as well as anyone," she said with some pride.

"I thought those days were gone. Don't you just buy a replacement body panel now?" I asked.

"Yes, for the regular work. But we specialize in working on collector and antique cars. It's the most profitable part of the business. Parts aren't easily available, so we have to repair and restore and even fabricate a lot of the panels."

I was nodding in admiration as I began to understand just how involved Charlie was in her business.

"Do you think that hinders your finding … dates … I mean … a guy?" I asked tentatively.

"I suppose. I've been so into the business in the past ten years since Dad got sick that I haven't given myself much of a chance for a personal life. Maybe that's why I'm not having much luck with my choices." She was looking off at the fireplace as she spoke, lost in her thoughts.

I reached over and covered her hand with mine without saying anything. She turned toward me and smiled, then leaned into me and kissed me lightly on the lips. I wasn't surprised. We had been heading in this direction since we met earlier. She trusted me and I desired her.

I reached back into my voluminous supply of clichés and asked, "Your place or mine?"

She snorted and chortled briefly as she composed herself. "Yours. If you can't cut it, I can just get up and leave."

"And if I can?"

"Well then … we can make other arrangements for the future," she said with crinkled smile.

I pulled her toward me and we kissed much more passionately. She was responding very nicely, I thought. I was looking forward to what would come next. We were pretty conspicuous out in the middle of the great room, so I rose and helped Charlie up from the sofa. We walked wordlessly back to my room, closing the door behind us.

Neither of us was interested in lingering over a sensuous undressing of each other. That was for another time. At this moment, we knew exactly what we wanted and both of us quickly stripped. I placed the small night table lamp on the floor and covered it with my shirt after switching it on. With all the other lights off, it provided a nice, softly-lit atmosphere as we slipped under the covers. We resumed our embrace from the sofa.

Charline was a big woman, but she wasn't fat. She was simply an oversized female with dramatic proportions. A large head with a prominent nose and a mass of curly blonde hair. Her eyes were a pale blue, her large mouth displaying an almost perfect set of white teeth. Big shoulders and big breasts, with large irregularly shaped areolas and prominent nipples.

Her rounded tummy featured a quarter-sized birthmark and a small navel cavity. She had trimmed and shaved her pubic hair to highlight her extended pink lips at the junction of her hefty thighs. She was truly all-woman, and a formidable challenge to me as I gazed at her voluptuous form.

"Foreplay?" I asked softly.

"No ... I'm too horny to wait."

I slipped my hand between her thighs and gently rubbed her outer lips, testing for lubrication. There was some, but not a lot, and so I carefully entered her with my index finger and massaged the opening to her vagina. In a matter of seconds, I felt the increase in wetness and I was satisfied it would be effortless if I was careful.

I invited her to guide me in and she quickly took me in hand, stroking the head of my cock over her now moistened labia and then moving me to her opening. Her hips arched upwards as she tried to pull me in. She wanted me inside her and she wanted me now.

As I pushed forward, I could feel her hands gripping my ass and pulling me in, demanding my full penetration. I began to relax and allowed her to set the pace. Within a few seconds she was telling me what she wanted.

"Faster, Lee! Harder! I need it harder!" she moaned.

I did what I could, still a bit worried about being too rough. She was thrashing about on the bed, her hands slapping my ass and then falling to her sides. I felt like a jockey riding a horse, but the horse had the whip. At some point, I let go and allowed myself to give in to her demands. If this was what she wanted, then I would give it to her for as long as I could.

Charlie was silent. She was grunting and sucking in air as I pounded into her, but saying nothing. Her head was rolling back and forth for a while until suddenly she stiffened, almost lifting her shoulders off the bed. A grunt and then a long, shuddering sigh signalled her orgasm. That was the trigger for me as well.

I rolled to the side with my arm fondling one lovely, big buttock. Charlie's eyes were closed, but she was still awake. She was breathing heavily and her hand reached out to caress my face. I heard a sigh of satisfaction accompanied by a smile as I waited for her recovery.

A couple of minutes later, her eyes opened and she smiled at me.

"Did that help?" I asked softly.

"Yes. That was a big help. I'm sorry if I was impatient. I really needed you to just ... fuck me. I didn't want a nice, slow, loving, sex session. I needed a good hard, old fashioned fucking."

I nodded my understanding.

"Does that put you off?" she asked carefully.

"Not at all," I assured her. "There's a time and a place for everything when it comes to sex."

"I'm glad you feel that way. I have some ... special needs. I hope they don't ... discourage you," she said, her eyes searching my face for a reaction.

"Tell me about them." I briefly wondered if I truly wanted to know everything.

"I like rough sex now and then. I'm a big girl and some men act a bit nervous around me. I like to be dominated by a man every so often, just to feel more like an ordinary woman."

"I can't bring myself to think of you as an ordinary woman. But I understand what you mean. What else?"

"Uhhhmmm ... I like anal sex. Not all the time, but it can be great with the right man." Again, she was tentative with her admission.

"Well, I don't have much experience, but ... I'm OK with that," I said. "And?" I continued.

"Uhhhmmm ... a little bondage?" She was obviously testing the water and seeing just how adventuresome I was willing to be.

"Oh ... well ... I have experienced a bit of that a long time ago with my wife, but nothing ... violent, you know."

"I like to be tied up and blindfolded. I like to pretend I'm a damsel in distress and that you are going to take me against my will. It's sort of a rape fantasy," she explained.

She was very unsure of how I was reacting to all this. To be truthful, I was very unsure of how I was reacting to it as well. On one hand, it sounded exciting. On the other, was it too kinky or depraved or even dangerous? I decided to let Charlie take the lead.

"Don't worry, Lee. I know you won't hurt me and it really turns me on. It isn't something I want to do every time. Just once in a while … you know … to keep things exciting?"

"I think I understand, but you'll have to make allowances for a poor city boy who's lived a sheltered life," I chuckled.

My humor lifted her doubts and she smiled back, reaching for me to pull me close. We held each other for a while until she turned to me again.

"You think you can help me put out the fire again?" she asked.

"I think I can … but just how would you like me to put out that fire?"

"Well, this is a ranch, and I do like to ride, so … why don't I saddle up?" she grinned.

"Your steed awaits." We were back to having fun. I always thought it was the best part of sex.

I was almost erect and Charlie looked after fixing that with her tongue, lips and fingers. She mounted me and slid effortlessly down on my again rigid cock and quickly began to stroke. I could have remained still, but with my hands on her hips I was involuntarily moving with her, revelling in the sensations.

I placed my hands on her lovely big breasts and began to knead them, running my thumbs over her nipples at the same time. That elicited a groan and a sigh from Charlie as she closed her eyes and surrendered to the sexual waves passing through her. Instead of the reckless abandon of our first joining, it was brimming in erotic intensity.

We carried on quite a while in this position, but remained dangling on the edge of the precipice. It was Charlie that broke the spell.

"Lee … I want to play a different game," she said breathlessly.

"Hmmm," was all I could manage.

"Let's play 'get along, little doggie,'" she said, looking down at me.

I must have had a quizzical look on my face until it dawned on me and I smiled.

She lifted off me and then crawled up over me until her sex was directly over my mouth. She lowered herself on me and I was quick to capture her clit in my lips and stroke it with my tongue. She responded immediately with a jolt and I felt her stiffen.

It was just a pit stop on the way to what she said she had wanted. She must have decided it was too good to pass up. I think she expected me to take my time before I went for the 'bull's-eye.' I heard her gasp and croak out a cry as I pressed my lips over the sensitive nub and dragged the raspy top of my tongue over the end. Having achieved the result I expected, I released her.

"Oh fuck ... that was a surprise," she gasped.

"Don't you like surprises," I chuckled.

"Love 'em," she said, still coming down from the shock of the sensation.

I slid out from underneath her and moved up behind her. She leaned back into me and my hands went automatically to her breasts. I gently squeezed and pinched them and Charlie squirmed in my embrace. Her head came back on her shoulder and I leaned forward to kiss her.

By now, my entry into her was effortless and we resumed our easy, rhythmic pace. I wasn't in any hurry to finish and the thrusts and moans Charlie responded with were the tell-tale that she was well into the zone. We could cruise like this for some time, I thought.

Charlie had other ideas, however. She began gripping my cock with her internal muscles and her push-back was becoming more insistent. I had a hunch what was coming and I was right.

"Harder, Lee! Do me, baby! Do me!"

I smiled as she began once more to pick up the pace, pleading for more action. I was only too happy to comply. This woman had big appetites. She enjoyed sex and made no bones about it. If we were going to become a couple for the next while, I was going to get a workout ... that was guaranteed.

I was hoping to last a little longer, and I was able to get Charlie off at least once more before we collapsed. We lay facing each other, breathing heavily from our exertions. I reached over and lightly pinched a nipple between the knuckles of my index and forefinger. My thumb stroked her areola and I could feel her nipple grow and respond. Her eyes flickered open and she smiled.

"I think we're going to be just fine together," she mumbled sleepily.

Who was I to argue?

My next conscious thought arrived sometime after six the next morning as I heard sounds from the kitchen and guessed that Francine and Lew were up. I looked over my shoulder at Charlie, still asleep at my back. I carefully extracted myself from the bed, picked up my bag and moved to the bathroom. Fifteen minutes later, I had showered, shaved and dressed. I slipped quietly out the door and padded down the hall toward the kitchen.

"Good morning," I said quietly as I walked in on Francine and Lew working in tandem, just as they had the previous afternoon.

"Hi ... you're up early," Francine said brightly.

"Anything I can do to help?"

"Sure ... if you'd like, you can set the table," Francine responded.

I set about my task after ascertaining the setting she wanted. It took less than ten minutes and I was back in the kitchen, accepting an offered coffee.

"So, you've made a new friend then?" Lew smiled.

"Yeah. So it seems," I grinned. "I think she was a bit lonely and down, but trying hard to hide it."

"You should have seen the jerk she brought. Movie star looks, movie star ego and no class ... not a speck," Francine said.

"We were pretty concerned for a while. It's the first time I've ever thought I was going to have to call in the cops to deal with a customer. Luckily, he was all talk and no action," Lew continued.

"Neither of us can figure out what Charlie was doing with a jerk like him," Francine said, shaking her head. "She's got more class in her little finger than that guy was ever going to have in a lifetime."

"She's a very different kind of woman, alright," I volunteered. "Smart, ambitious, talented."

"You forgot good-looking and sexy," Francine laughed.

"Oh no I didn't. I was just trying to be a gentleman for a change," I kidded.

"Who are you guys talking about," a sleepy voice came from behind me. Charlie shuffled into the kitchen. She had obviously gone up to her room to get a change of clothes and was dressed in shorts and a baggy t-shirt.

"You, of course," Lew and I chorused. That brought about more laughter.

Charlie strolled up behind me, wrapping her arms around me and hanging her chin on my shoulder.

"I have an announcement," Charlie said, smiling over my shoulder. "Mr. Dickhead has been replaced. I'm pleased to introduce my new good friend," she paused. "What did you say your name was?"

Another round of laughs. I turned my head and gave her a good morning kiss on the cheek.

"Smart move, Charlie. This one comes with references," Francine bantered.

It was a light, fun mood in the kitchen. All the while, preparations for breakfast were continuing. It was also plain that Charlie and Francine had become friends. Their playful sparring was unforced and dissolved any possible tension from that first day. The fact that Charlie and I had become lovers was accepted without comment.

I found gainful employment in the barn that morning. I needed it. The breakfast was fabulous and I made a pig of myself. I figured some strenuous exercise would be the only way I could even face the prospect of more food before the evening.

The back of the lodge faced toward the old buildings of the ghost town and the large swimming pool took up most of the area behind my room and the kitchen. I had volunteered to help move some hay from the loft to the ground floor of the barn. Any grass in the large, fenced paddocks had long since burned off and hay was the order of the day, along with the twice-a-day ration of oats and other feed supplements.

The horses were an expensive asset and they had to be cared for regularly. A vet called in at the lodge every month, just to review the health of nearly thirty animals. Each afternoon featured a trail ride to one of the many locations nearby, including a lake, a forested area, the cattle range, and some rolling sagebrush-strewn hills to the west. There were plenty of streams, so even the hot weather of summer could be managed as long as the horses were well-watered and not ridden hard.

Stripped to the waist, I was soaked in sweat by noon, with prickly bits of hay irritating my skin. I had moved almost a hundred bales. More than needed, but I had filled the day-feed pen. It felt good to be active, but I expected my muscles would be sore from the unaccustomed effort.

The pool looked too good to pass up and I slipped into my room, showered quickly, donned my trunks and returned to the pool for a swim. It was the perfect answer. I was standing on the bottom along the side, up to my shoulders in water when I felt a soft pair of hands clasp my head. I didn't need to guess who it was.

"Hi Charlie."

"Hi Lee. Are you all finished with your work?"

"Yup. There's enough hay there for the rest of the week. I've earned my lunch."

"You've earned more than that," she said seductively.

"Hmmmm … whatcha got in mind?" I knew perfectly well what she had in mind.

"How about a nice siesta after lunch and then maybe we can go for a ride by the lake," she said in that same sexy voice.

"Will I get much rest during my siesta?"

"No chance in hell," she laughed.

"I didn't think so. Well, I guess we all have to make sacrifices."

I demonstrated a great deal of restraint at the barbeque luncheon. I had a hot dog, a tossed salad and a beer. I was still working off my excess from breakfast. I'm glad I did. Charlie had a full schedule planned for siesta, and I was the main course.

I had no illusions that I was falling in love. This was lust, friendship, but nothing more. On the other hand, Charlie wasn't expecting anything either. She wanted to feel good and feel wanted. I had the sense that it had been some time since someone … anyone … had made an effort to make her feel desired. It was something I could do without a second thought. I found her enormously sexy and open. She was another in the recent parade of women who had restored my ego and self confidence.

Our "afternoon delight" was slow, sensuous and interrupted by little rests. Touching, kissing, talking softly, watching and learning what pleased each other. It may have been the perfect siesta after all. When we rose, it was nearly three. We put on our swimwear, holding hands as we strolled to the pool. The ride could wait for another day.

Before and after dinner, I resumed my role as a bartender and Charlie and I had a chance to spend some time with the German couple. They were a bit shy, primarily because they were uncertain of their language skills. They needn't have been. We had no problem understanding them. In typically direct Teutonic fashion, they asked about Charlie's original "escort." We laughed as he was dismissed from our thoughts. In equally characteristic European fashion, my liaison with Charlie was accepted as nothing unusual.

As he did the previous evening, Lew turned on some music and several couples began to dance. We danced of course. This evening we held each other closely, not worrying about appearances. I was confident we were acknowledged as a couple. An hour into the evening, Francine and Lew joined us on the dance floor. They may have been the hosts, but they were also a couple. I was feeling very good about this week.

We retired a little earlier than the previous night, this time to her room. I suspected Charlie had a plan and I was intrigued with what it might be. I didn't have long to wait.

"Lee ... you remember we talked about my ... fantasies ... the things I like to do ... now and then?" she said haltingly.

I laughed. Of course I remembered. "Okay, Charlie, what's on the menu tonight?"

"I have this thing ... I told you about it ... I like to be tied up and blindfolded," she continued carefully. "Are you all right with that?"

"I'm okay if you are. But you don't sound very confident," I suggested.

"I guess I'm more worried about you ... I mean ... how you'll react to it."

"You know I won't hurt you, babe," I said quietly. "What do you want me to do?"

"I want you to tie me up ... spread eagle fashion ... and then ... I want you to fuck me like you were raping me." She was almost whispering. She was still very unsure how I would respond to this.

"I won't be able to see or touch you. I won't know what to expect, except that I know I'm going to be raped by a very powerful man. Can you do that?"

"I don't know. I've never raped a woman before. I don't know how," I confessed.

"Lee … I trust you … just be the powerful lover I know you are. I can imagine the rest. It's a fantasy … not real. I want you to try to imagine that you are my conqueror … that you can do anything you want to me. Torture me, beat me, fuck me, kill me … anything."

She reached down beside the bed and produced some silk scarves from a canvas tote bag. There was also a black bandana which I took to be the mask. Charlie showed me how to tie the scarves so that a single pull on the end would release them. I felt better about that, but not much. The mask was made of soft material with Velcro to fasten it.

She lay back on the bed and smiled at me. It helped to relieve some of my uncertainty. I tied her ankles to the vertical ribs of the footboard first, then her wrists to the headboard. She was naked and completely vulnerable. I was still uncomfortable about this.

Charlie raised her head and told me to wrap the mask around her, covering her eyes. I did, making sure it wasn't too tight. Again, I could remove it with a single pull. I stood beside the bed as I finished and gazed at this magnificent woman in her helpless state. I had to admit it was an erotic sight and it was causing me to become aroused.

"Please don't hurt me." I was a plaintive cry from Charlie. It took me a moment to understand this was part of the fantasy. It was my turn to play.

"Shut up!" I snarled. Two can play this game, I decided. "You don't get a say … this is my party, bitch!" I hoped I hadn't overdone it.

"Please … please … what are you going to do to me?" she pleaded in a convincingly frightened voice.

"I've decided to change the script, lady. I've decided to torture you before I fuck you," I snarled. I was a spontaneous decision I had made on my own. I knew what I wanted to do. I hoped it would be fun for her.

"Oh god, no. Not torture. Please …," she cried.

"There's no point in crying about it. It's going to happen. I'm going to make you suffer," I spat in my best Snidely Whiplash voice. This was going to be quite different.

I stood quietly beside the bed and then in a moment of inspiration, I walked quietly around to the other side, hoping that she couldn't hear me. I leaned over and took her right nipple into my mouth and first sucked on it, and then nipped at it with my teeth. She stiffened and then jolted at my nip. A soft cry escaped her.

My next move was to take two of her toes into my mouth and use my tongue to stimulate them. She reacted. She hadn't expected this. I could see a smile on her lips as she began to appreciate my "torture." I moved softly around the bed again and this time placed a kiss on her lips, waiting for her to open to me. When she did, I immediately withdrew and moved to her lovely thighs. I used my tongue along the inside of each and she reacted immediately. Her back arched and I could hear her gasp as I used my lips on her upper thighs, close but not touching her sex.

Next, back to her breast, teasing the areola and nipple with my tongue and teeth as she writhed in reaction. I was beginning to understand what was happening. She couldn't see, and everything was unexpected. Only her sense of touch and hearing was in play, and her hearing wasn't helping her much.

In a moment of inspiration, I moved back up her body. My cock was fully erect and I moved to put it on her lips. It took her a moment to understand what it was that she was feeling and tasting. I could see her smile as she turned her head and took the head of my cock in her mouth and bathed it with her tongue and lips. She was having too much fun. I withdrew and she groaned when I did.

"This is torture, remember. I control you for my pleasure … not yours," I said in my most sinister voice.

My mouth dipped to her now sodden pussy and with a single long lick, I stroked her swollen lips from bottom to top. She squealed and her hips snapped upward in response. Once would be enough. I moved to the other side and resumed my attack on her breast, then down once more to her toes and then thighs. She was squirming now. I could hear her breathing becoming more rapid. It was exciting her and I was encouraged.

Again, I gave her a taste of my cock, now spilling pre-cum from the tip. She recognized the scent and taste and hungrily took it into her mouth. Once again, however, I withdrew it before she could achieve any sense of satisfaction. She moaned and I heard a "no" escape her lips.

I laughed as nasty a laugh as I could create. I surprised myself. I was enjoying this in some perverse way. I went back to her lovely delta and began to tease her once more. She was now in a state of constant motion. Her hips were undulating, almost begging for a cock. Her head rolled back and forth and it clearly took all her self-control not to plead for relief.

I backed off once again and silently waited, standing by the bedside as she continued to squirm, not knowing what would come next. I wanted to bring her as close to an orgasm as I could without allowing her to complete it.

"Please, please …," she moaned.

"Don't waste your breath. I'll do what I want to … when I want to … and there isn't a damn thing you can do about it," I chortled in my faked evil voice.

She was very agitated now as it had been a couple of minutes since I had last touched her. I decided it was time for the big finish. I silently moved beside her, and taking my index finger, ran it upward from her anus to her clit, barely touching her as I did.

"Yahhhhhhh … oh god… oh please!" She had responded violently and immediately to my delicate touch.

I repeated the move … then again a few seconds later … then a fourth time. Each time she gasped and reacted to my faint touch. This truly was torture and I wondered if I wasn't enjoying this more than I should. It was time to bring her to the brink. The next time, I poked my fingertip into her ass and then rimmed her with it before dragging it slowly up her perineum toward her now fully flooded sex.

I moved silently to the other side of the bed and pressed my forefinger into her pussy, slowly but surely. I bent over her and gently blew on her glistening lips as they absorbed first one finger and then a second. I hooked them slowly upward, searching for her G spot and dragging the pads along the roof of her vagina.

Charlie had become a perpetual motion machine. She writhed and squirmed and twisted against her restraints, all the while mewling in frustration. Her breathing had quickened, and I had to guess when the right time would come for me to release her from this torture.

I removed my fingers and began to aggressively lick and stroke her pussy with my tongue. Charlie was now in a state of total arousal. The time had come. I mounted the bed, moved between her legs and presented my cock to her now saturated entrance. She pushed her body upward, attempting to impale herself on my rigid member. I pulled back, denying her that pleasure until she could stand no more of this teasing.

I allowed her to find me and then, in a single, powerful stroke, I entered her. A cry of something unearthly escaped as I drove into her and we were joined. She shuddered violently at that first stroke and I knew she had orgasmed at that very moment.

"Time for your punishment, woman," I grunted.

There was no response other than a sigh of what I took to be released. It was time to act and I began to drive myself into her in powerful, long strokes. She was crying out in what I could only assume was ecstasy. It certainly wasn't pain or rejection. I continued to drive into her hard and fast. I lost myself in this strange new pleasure. I had joined her in this fantasy, punishing her with pleasure.

It ended in a fury of gasping, grunts, and cries. As I slipped off her inert form, I pulled the end of the silk ties from her hands and then her feet. I left the mask just as it was. She hadn't moved other than to allow her arms to flop by her side.

"I'm going now ... but I'll be back. You just won't know when," I growled quietly.

I rose from the bed and gazed at her unmoving form. She continued to breathe deeply, her eyes still covered. I leaned over and kissed her softly on the lips and then moved to the ensuite. When I returned, she had removed the mask and her head was propped up on the pillows, watching me silently. I began to worry that I had carried my game too far.

"Where the hell did that come from?" she eventually croaked.

I moved to the side of the bed and sat, my hand reaching for her face.

"I'm not sure. I just thought ... I'm sorry ... I thought that if I was ... unpredictable ... if you didn't know what might happen next. Well, I'm sorry. I won't do that again," I said meekly.

"Why? It was incredible. I've never been more aroused in my life. When you finally entered me, the orgasm was instantaneous and it was fucking mind-blowing!"

I breathed a sigh of relief. She wasn't upset. She was surprised. I hadn't given her what she thought she wanted, but it worked out just as well anyway.

"Who was that guy?" she asked with a smile.

"Snidely Whiplash," I snorted. "And you were Little Nell. This time there wasn't any Dudley Do-Right around to save you."

"Somehow I don't think I fit the description of Little Nell. I'm just not that little." She looked at me with a sly grin. "But you … you are a perfect Snidely Whiplash. Rotten to the core. Willing to torture women and have your wicked way with them. My kind of guy!" she laughed.

I lay down beside her, both of us naked, both of us sated for now and both of us still coming down from an extraordinary high. As I thought about it, I enjoyed my role, now even more so when I was sure Charlie had as well.

"Can we do that again?" she asked, teasing me with her fingers on my chest.

"We'll see. You don't want me to repeat the same thing again. I'll have to come up with something different … something even more … diabolical," I growled.

"Ahhhhh … diabolical sounds good," she smiled.

"I'm going to have to put you on rationing. No more than once a week, maybe even less," I said. "It would get a little stale after a while and I'd have a hard time finding new, safe things to do."

"Maybe I don't want safe." This caught me a bit off guard, since she said in what I took to be a serious tone.

"You don't mean that. I won't do anything that would harm you … physically or mentally," I said firmly.

"I know. I know you wouldn't. I was just thinking out loud. It was so exciting … so different. The reward was amazing. I know I want more."

"I'm sure you do. You have to make sure you know where the limits are. More importantly, you have to know and trust your partner. I mean, completely trust," I emphasized.

"I trust you, Lee. Completely. If … if you wanted to stay … I mean after this vacation … if you wanted to be with me …." She ended her offer as her voice tailed off.

"I've thought about it, Charlie. I honestly have. We've come together so fast and so …." I was struggling for what I wanted to say.

"It's too soon to make a big decision like that, Charlie. Why don't we just enjoy what we have now? We've got almost two more weeks to decide what comes next. You've been hurt too many times to just leap into another relationship without giving yourself time to know what you actually want." I was stalling for myself as well.

The balance of Charlie's vacation passed far too quickly. We spent almost every hour together and we were comfortable in each other's company. Since I had begun this journey in March, I had not spent as much time with any one person as I had with her and it gave me the opportunity to examine my own motives and desires.

She was a powerful woman and a wonderful lover. She reintroduced me to anal sex, and while it was something that I only occasionally wanted, it was enormously sensual, and according to Charlie, something I was good at. My only technique was to go slowly, use plenty of lube and try desperately not to hurt her. That apparently was enough.

We did try the bondage game once more, this time with some variations that I had thought of beforehand. I used a feather and one of her dildos. I tied her face down on the bed, ankles close together with enough length to allow her to rise on her knees. She could manage to get her breasts off the bed far enough that I could play with them as I "tortured" her.

My big finish was prefaced by a careful insertion of the dildo into her ass, using plenty of KY jelly. After using the feather to tease her to distraction, the dildo was almost a relief. However, when I pushed into her pussy from behind, she could feel my cock and the dildo at the same time and it sent her off almost as violently as before. I finished with a driving fuck that had her crying out her satisfaction and ultimately collapsing on the bed.

On our last night together, we made love. I knew that I wasn't in love with Charlie, and I think she knew that too. But we had become very close and our intimacy was almost like being in love. Of all my experiences in the past five months, this amazing interlude would help push me toward my ultimate realization. I was near to the decision that my rehabilitation was over.

Charlie did everything she could think of to convince me to come back to Toronto with her. I was tempted. She was a powerful woman and the sex was fabulous, but that's what it was sex. My temptation to go with her was fueled by my desire to see her happy and in the arms of a man who would treat her with respect and devotion. She deserved nothing less.

She was good about it. There were no tears, no bitterness, and no regrets. She knew it would probably end this way, but tried mightily to delay the inevitable. The last morning, she kissed me goodbye as she boarded the shuttle to Kamloops and the return to her normal life. We had promised to keep in touch and I thought we probably would. We were certainly friends, and friends stay in touch.

The next group of vacationers arrived that afternoon and I tried to go back to some kind of routine. I had found a number of small jobs that I could contribute, but with Charlie gone, I was now a "freeloader" on Lew and Francine's hospitality. I was also lonely again. I realized how much I had come to depend on Charlie's companionship, particularly at night. I wondered briefly if I should have returned with her. I knew the truth, though. It wouldn't have worked … at least not in the long term.

I lounged in the pool on Sunday afternoon. It was overcast and I had the place to myself. The new crop was all excited about their first trail ride and had ridden off to the sagebrush hills for an afternoon jaunt.

Lew, Francine and I had finished making the beds and cleaning the bathrooms. Francine was puttering about in the kitchen, organizing herself for the evening meal. Lew was in the barn, checking on the feed supplies and making sure all the equipment was in working order. I was lost in thought as I leaned against the side wall of the pool, the warm water up to my neck.

I was going to accept Harold Sinden's offer of a job with Orca Investigations. I still had to pass all the required evaluations and training, but in talking to my friend Pete Dennison, I was confident I could manage that.

So what was bothering me? Was it Charlie? Did I need more time? I didn't think so. I couldn't put my finger on it. Something was missing. Something buried inside me that I couldn't quite reach. It was frustrating. I wanted a key to unlock that compartment. I waded out of the pool, dried myself and headed for my room. Perhaps an afternoon nap would clear my head.

I slept fitfully for an hour or so before rising and wandering down to the kitchen to see if I could help. Francine was by herself, putting the finishing touches on four large pies. I watched as she effortlessly worked, preparing them for the oven.

"Did you get some sleep?" she asked, not looking at me.

"A bit … maybe an hour."

She turned and looked at me, a frown on her face.

"What's the problem? Missing Charlie?"

"I suppose. I knew it would end this way, but … just the same, it was nice while it lasted," I admitted.

"So … what comes next?" She had returned to her task.

"I truly don't know. I think I'm close to ending this adventure and going back to work, but … something's not quite settled yet."

"Hmmmph," was her only comment.

"What's that mean," I chuckled.

She stopped what she was doing and turned to me. Whatever was on her mind was serious.

"You've been lonely for a long time, Lee. Even before your divorce. Lew told me about the women, the ones you've been meeting on this trip … what do you think they mean?"

I thought about her question and hesitated. "I suppose they were a way of restoring my pride … my ego … my self-confidence." It was the most honest answer I could summon.

"And have they?"

"Pretty much. I feel more confident. I don't feel guilty. I don't feel like I've taken advantage of them," I answered defensively.

"Good. Your conscience is clear. So, I repeat … what's next?"

"Start over, I guess. I really don't know. Everything that's happened to me on this trip is almost … like a dream. I have a hard time believing it's all real."

"Oh, it's real alright," she grinned. "Let me ask you a question. If all those women are still available and you could go back and do it all again … who would be your first choice?"

"That's not fair. I've just seen Charlie leave and the others are weeks or even months in my past. I don't know if I can honestly answer that," I admitted.

She looked at me with a level gaze. "I had to make that decision. I left a bad marriage and for some time I searched, trying to find something ... someone ... better for myself. When I found Lew, I knew. I don't know how ... but I knew. And I was right."

She continued to look at me with an unflinching gaze. I could only nod my understanding.

I poured myself a coffee and walked into the great room, dropping into an overstuffed armchair, thinking about her comments. I put my head back and went through the last months in my mind. Who were these women I had so easily engaged? Which of them would be the most compatible with my ... heart? Which of them would challenge me? Which of them would excite me? Which of them would accept me ... as I am?

I must have drifted off and I awoke when the first of the trail riders stomped into the room. I had been dreaming about Francine's question and now I was pretty sure I had the answer. I picked up the cold coffee and put it on the bar. As I stood there, it became clearer. I knew, for the first time, what this whole trip had been about. Francine's simple question had framed it all. It was a matter of making choices with no guarantees. Nothing ventured, nothing gained.

I walked into my room and opened my bag, searching for the means to my next move. I found what I was looking for, picked up my cell phone from the night table and turned it on. I punched in the number and listened for the ring tone, hoping it wouldn't cut to voice mail. It didn't.

"Hi ... it's Lee Stephenson."

I had time to think now and that's what I did. It would be five hours before I would arrive at my destination. As I drove, I kept coming back to the same question. Why her? What was it about her that separated her from all the others? Why was I so certain it had to be her?

I had been wandering aimlessly for almost six months, trying to forget my failed marriage and at the same time, trying to find a new life. There was a job waiting for me, so it was just a matter of coming to terms with what I really wanted for my personal future.

It wasn't that difficult to define. I wanted a companion, a woman to share my life. But more than anything, I wanted love. I wanted that elusive, undefined intangible almost every person seeks – love. I thought back over the wonderful women I had met on my travels.

Constance, the elegant, sensual, mature woman of the world who had first introduced me to my new life.

Glynnis, the young, spirited, small-town girl with ambition and the desire for a full life with a certain young doctor.

Sophia, the sophisticated ex-model. Darkly quiet and mysterious, seeking out liaisons with men for both herself and her mother.

Then Pattie. The fun, self-assured, ambitious young woman who had shared my bed and berth on the Shushwap houseboat. I would probably be seeing her again at Orca Investigations.

And Charlie. The woman I had spent the most time with on this wandering voyage of self-discovery. Charlie with the large and varied sexual appetite. Talented Charlie, running her own business and trying to get a grip on her personal life. She was the catalyst for my understanding of this journey. She and Francine had helped me bring my life into focus. I now knew what I wanted from my future.

But, in the end, it was Beth. Beth, the accomplished artist who needed someone to push her to realize her capabilities. Big beautiful Beth, the fascinating, voluptuous redhead, staying in a high-class time-share courtesy of an unknown "sugar daddy." We had made a connection too. She was so much more challenging than the others. I found I was much more outspoken around her, even daring her to become a more complete artist.

Perhaps it was because she appeared unreachable. Too beautiful? Certainly desired by every man who saw her. Insecure? Thinking she intimidated men. There was likely a lot of truth in that belief. Yet, in my arrogance, I always believed she was attainable. I never once thought that I didn't belong with her. Why? What was it about her that made me believe in myself?

Our conversation on the phone had been brief, but intense.

"Lee, how wonderful to hear from you. Where are you?"

"Kamloops. I'm just packing up and getting ready to come back. I think I've done what I needed to do."

"Good. I'm glad. Can you come here … to my place?" she asked tentatively.

"Yes. I can. I want to. You're the reason I'm coming back home. I wanted to see you again … to talk to you … about us," I said hesitantly. I must surely have sounded hopeful. I wished I had sounded more confident.

"About us?" She paused. "Yes … that's a good idea. When will you be here?" She sounded calm and unruffled by my direct request.

"I should be there about six. Why don't we plan on dinner together?"

"Fine … but I don't want to go out. We'll have it here … where we can talk … privately," she said quietly. I wasn't positive, but it sounded like there was a hint of happiness in that lovely, soft voice.

"I'll pick up a bottle of wine along the way, and I won't be late."

=The End=

Here is a sample from another story you may enjoy:

DEXTER'S
Renaissance

LEE NORTH

Hot Romance Erotica

That May picnic was the beginning of a series of dates that Michelle and I enjoyed. Sometimes to a movie or play, often for dinner, occasionally for a ballgame. It was on one of those dates that there was a distinct shift in our relationship. Until then, we had held hands, kissed lightly, and generally behaved ourselves. I think we both could feel the pressure building. It changed after we had spent a pleasant evening at a local play.

We were in her late model Lincoln and I was driving. In the past, I would stop at the Rossmoor and she would drive on to her apartment. That night she had other ideas.

"Drive to my place, Dex. It's Friday, and we've got all weekend. You haven't been to my place yet and I'd like to spend some time with you," she said, placing her hand over mine.

It didn't take me any time at all to agree and head toward Lakeshore Drive. As we neared the building, Michelle took a small transmitter from her purse and pushed a button. The open grilled gate began to rise and I drove into the underground parking area as she directed me to her numbered space. The transmitter also unlocked the door to the elevator and stairs. After waiting a moment for an available car, a door slid open and we entered with Michelle inserting a card and pushing a button marked "R."

When we stepped out of the car, a large glass window was directly in front of us and I could see we were at the top of the building. To the left was 2102 and to the right, 2101. Michelle guided me right and opened the door, stepping in and turning on some lights. It was a very nice and apparently large penthouse suite, one of two on the top floor of the building. As I looked around I saw the trappings of affluence; fine furniture, interesting artwork, and lush carpeting. Michelle kicked off her shoes and I followed suit.

"Dex, I'm all sticky from the humidity today. I'm going to have a shower and change. Why don't you do the same, then we can relax and get to know each other better," she smiled.

I wasn't about to decline the offer and happily agreed. She led me to the main bathroom, handed me some towels and a washcloth and told me how to work the controls on the shower system. I needed the lesson. It was a multi-head system with pre-selected temperatures. The cabinet itself was almost as big as the bathroom in my apartment.

As I soaped and rinsed, I almost expected that Michelle would suddenly appear and join me, but that didn't happen. I stepped out of the shower, towelled myself off, and dressed in my slacks and shirt. I didn't bother with socks. They wouldn't be as fresh as I was so I stuffed them in my back pocket as I headed barefoot for the living area.

Waiting for Michelle, I wandered about the spacious penthouse. There was a dining area with a very nice buffet and china cabinet, along with a large period-style table and chairs. The kitchen was through a wide passage and it too was large, with a big island and plenty of cabinet and counter space. Most houses didn't have this much room.

I was just coming out of my inspection of the kitchen when Michelle reappeared and got my undivided attention. She was wearing a black silk pyjama suit, if that's what it's called. It was floor length, very sleek with material flowing from its wide legs and arms. She had a smile for me as she approached, then stopped and swirled in a circle to emphasize the graceful lines of her attire.

"You like?" she asked, already knowing my answer.

"Very nice … very elegant." I almost added very sexy. As she had moved to show off the garment it was immediately apparent that she was wearing nothing beneath it. Her nipples protruded clearly in front and her buttocks were perfectly outlined in back. I could feel my erection beginning to develop.

"Would you care for coffee … or perhaps a glass of wine or brandy?" she asked in a tempting tone.

"I'd like a glass of brandy, please."

"Oh, good. I'll have one too," she said, turning to move into the kitchen.

I followed her as if she was drawing me along. Perhaps it was the magnetic appeal of her, dressed as she was in such alluring garb. She reached up in a cupboard for the brandy bottle and I stepped behind her to help her. I was directly behind her now, touching her slightly with my hips and chest. On the spur of the moment, I did something I would never have thought I would do. With the fingertips of my right hand, I lightly, slowly, ran them up her side, feeling her ribs as I went. Then, in a moment of complete recklessness, I moved my hand and gently cupped and stroked a fulsome breast. I felt her shiver from the contact but she didn't push me away or resist my touch. In fact, I was sure I heard a soft moan.

I couldn't see her face, but she had begun to lean back into me, the brandy bottle now forgotten. Her hands were on the countertop as if bracing her against an assault. My left hand joined the right in teasing her nipples and now her groan was more audible. Emboldened, I allowed my left hand to slip down over her abdomen and softly rub the silky smooth material of her gown.

I felt her backside push slowly back into me and she could certainly now feel my erection. I moved my hips to place my hardened member between her cheeks. She welcomed that with a swaying motion that only reinforced my hardness. One of us was going to have to do something soon.

It was Michelle who took my right hand and guided it inside her top, giving me access to her breasts. She pulled at the fold of the material and I felt a little pop as a small snap released the upper half of the garment. Still holding my hand, she slid it down to her waist where another small snap gave way and the gown parted completely. I felt her shrug her shoulders and the lovely black item fell at her feet. She was naked before me, still facing away but leaning back more urgently against me, pressing herself into my prominent manhood. Once more, I did something I would not have thought I could attempt. I intimated with my knee that I wanted her to spread her legs and she immediately complied. She understood exactly what I was intending.

I unbuttoned my pants and they too fell at my feet, my briefs following them almost immediately. I took my cock in my hand and began to stroke her already wet centre in preparation for my entry. Again, she did everything she could to help me and within a few moments I was pushing into her. Slowly and carefully at first, but her insistence gave me courage to thrust a little more and soon I was buried well inside her.

I moved a little more forcefully and quickly as she continued to encourage me. There was absolutely no doubt in my mind that this was what she had planned all along. Her voice soon joined the action, not so much with words but with little cries of encouragement and pleasure. How long it had been since she had been with a man I did not know. I only knew she was with me now, and I was reaping the reward of her pent up need.

I leaned my head forward and captured an earlobe between my lips, then licked the back of her neck as I continued to stroke into her. In response, she threw her head back, growling a pagan, earthy moan of lust, slamming her ass back into me, the smacking sound of our joining now growing louder. This was probably going to end quite soon, but I did whatever I could to hold off as long as possible. A few moments later, her moves became more erratic and we almost fell out of rhythm as she began her orgasmic journey. I stayed with her as long as I could, but I was going to finish as well and there was nothing I could do to prevent it. I felt myself release into her once, twice, then a third time. As I did, she sagged against me and I wrapped my arms around her waist so that she didn't collapse against the granite counter or on the floor.

In all my experience, limited as it might have been, I had never had a more erotic, spontaneous coupling than this. I was in no condition to continue. Michelle was leaning back into me, breathing heavily and holding my arms tightly as they encircled her. Not a word had passed between us from the time she walked to the liquor cupboard.

I'm still not sure what got into me that night. I was either very confident of myself or very reckless. Probably the latter. Nonetheless, I picked the naked beauty up in my arms and carefully steered my way out of the kitchen toward the master bedroom.

When I arrived, I saw that the bed had been turned down and I carefully laid Michelle on it crosswise with her legs dangling over the side. Her eyes were open and she was staring at me, no doubt wondering what I was doing. Still, neither of us had yet spoken.

I pulled off my shirt and now as naked as she, I got on my knees on the lushly carpeted floor, my hands gently but insistently pushing her legs apart. Again, she offered no resistance. I moved between her thighs and began to kiss the flawless, smooth skin. I was about to work my way up to the place where I had just planted my seed when I felt her hands in my hair. Was this a 'stop' or a 'go?' I could see a bit of my semen on the lips of her vagina and I wondered what possessed me to try this. What was I trying to prove? Yet, even with that question in my head, I continued. As Michelle realized what I was planning, she must have had second thoughts. That had prompted her to place her hands on my head again, trying to decide if she should put a stop to my intentions. As I made up my mind to continue, I felt her resistance lessen.

I moved toward my target and slowly, with the flat of my tongue, I began to make love to her once again. This was going to be a very different kind of penetration. I had plenty of experience with oral sex but none just after I had planted my seed inside a woman. It was too late to stop now, and Michelle was making no sign that she wanted me to. In fact, I was bringing her back to life with my tongue and fingers. Her hips were rising and falling erratically, responding to whatever stimuli she felt. Her grip on my head tightened and I could feel her fingers in my hair. She was holding on tight, her body dancing to whatever music my tongue created. I flicked the tip of her clitoris and got the response I expected. Her hips snapped up in reaction.

I was beginning to tire … or at least my tongue was. Michelle was nearing another orgasm and I willed myself to continue. At last she let go and I could stop and rest. I crawled up beside her, lying on my back. She rolled over me and gave me a deep, soulful kiss. Whatever I had accomplished, she approved of it. I wondered if it was something her late husband had not provided.

We lay there for a while, her head on my shoulder, our legs dangling over the edge of the bed. I kissed her forehead and ran my fingers through her soft, flowing hair. Her hand was holding my now flaccid cock, not manipulating it, just holding it lightly.

"That was wonderful," she said at last. "I didn't realize just how much I wanted you and you were perfect for me."

"We took some chances tonight," I said. "That gown didn't leave much to the imagination."

"It was either that or I would just come out naked. It was a coin toss."

"Were you worried I wouldn't get the message?"

"That thought did cross my mind. I can never be sure just what you are thinking about when it comes to women, Dex. Sometimes shy, but tonight a completely different person. You took command and I was the lucky one when you did."

"You were irresistible. I'm sure that was your plan, wasn't it? Well, it worked. I couldn't resist you, so everything that happened was a result of that."

"You'll stay tonight, won't you?"

"Yes. You might regret it in the morning, but I do want to stay. I want to wake up with you."

"We've started something, haven't we?" It was as much a statement as a question.

"I hope so. Is that what you want?" I wondered.

"Yes. As little as I know about you, as little time as I've known you, everything I've learned tells me that you are right for me."

"Well, we're going to have some time to find out so let's enjoy ourselves and see where it goes. I'm not a one-night-stand kind of guy. I'm looking for something more than that."

"You wouldn't be in this apartment tonight if I thought otherwise. But now that you're here, I'm going to keep you here as long as I can."

After a few minutes, Michelle rose and padded to the ensuite bathroom, closing the door behind her. She returned a minute or so later and crawled on top of me, rubbing my still limp cock with her lightly haired sex. I began to respond to her tantalizing little game and she noticed.

"Oh … isn't that nice. Can I have some more please, sir?"

"Of course you may. Just tell me your heart's desire, young lady, and I'll try and fulfill your wishes."

"Well, after that glorious fucking you gave me in the kitchen, I think I'd like you to make love to me. Something nice and slow and lasting."

"How would you like me to start? A little foreplay, perhaps?"

If you enjoyed this sample then look for **Dexter's Renaissance**.

Here is another sample you may also enjoy:

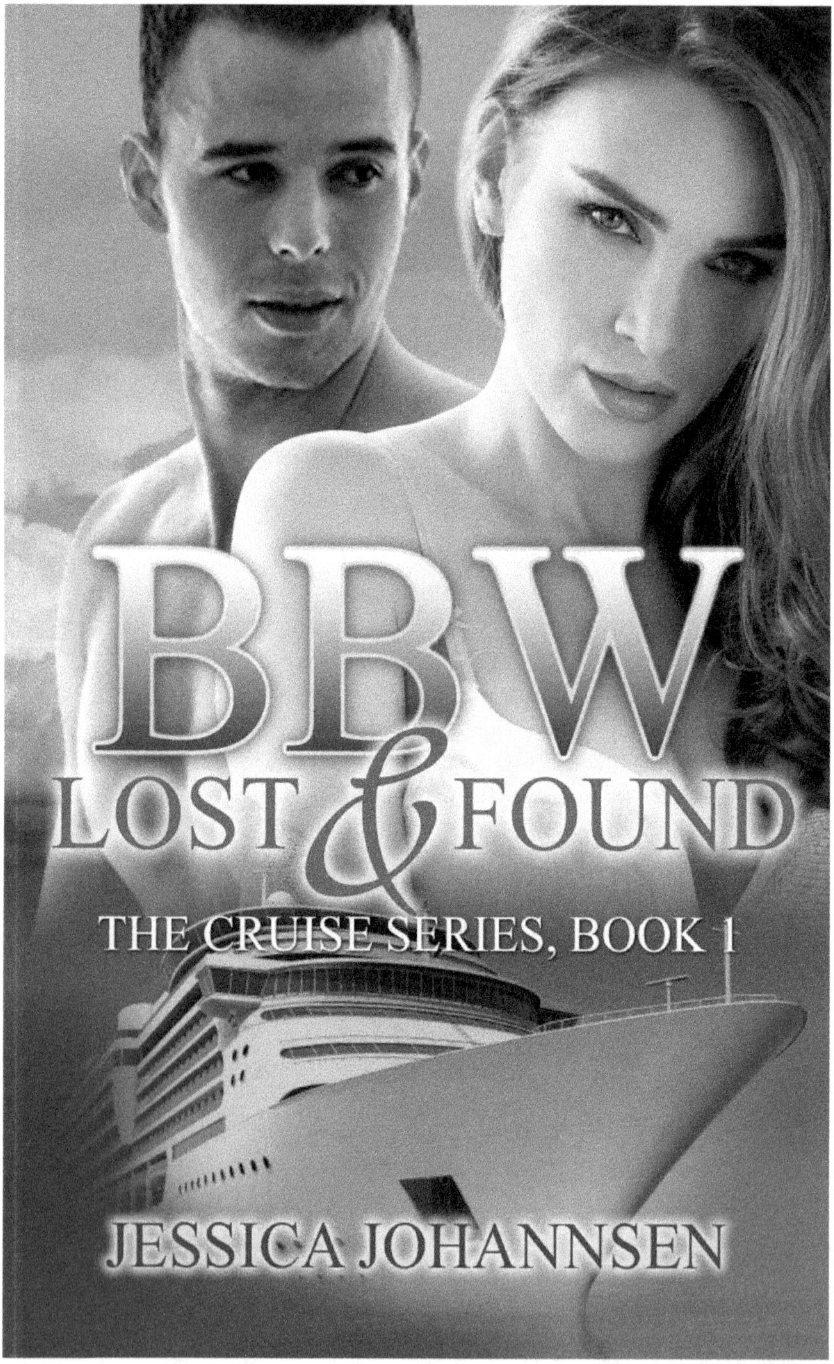
BBW
LOST & FOUND
THE CRUISE SERIES, BOOK 1
JESSICA JOHANNSEN

If Belinda weren't staring right at it, she never would have believed that it could be true. As Belinda peered down at the computer screen, the woman in the photo seemed to stare right back. The woman's casual grin made Belinda feel mocked; made her feel as though the woman flaunted what she possessed.

Belinda covered her mouth with both hands to contain the scream that built in her throat. The young, sexy blond was her husband's mistress; the pictures on his computer finally answered the question that she had been too afraid to ask. No, it wasn't her imagination; their marriage of fifteen years had finally passed the point of no return. She knew she had to finish getting ready for work. Sitting here at her husband's desk, wearing only a bra and skirt, she felt open, exposed, and raw.

Belinda searched the contents of her husband's hard drive, finding album after album of photos. There were hundreds of pictures of the mistress, in every state of dress and undress. Skipping back to the earliest album, she checked the upload date. Her stomach lurched when she realized that the first pictures were dated over a year ago. Almost to the day that her husband had moved out of their bedroom and taken up permanent residence in the den.

Belinda wound her long black hair up into the bun that she wore for work. She applied make-up; she puckered and blew a kiss to her reflection, a silly habit. She flinched, realizing that many of the photos her husband kept were pictures of the blond woman making just that face, the wink and kiss.

Tears threatened to fall. She closed her eyes and took a deep breath. He had already ruined their marriage; she would not let him ruin her meeting with the board.

Belinda turned her mind to work, making sure she arrived in the conference room before anyone else. She set about preparing the screen. When Mr. Whiting entered the room, she was standing at the podium, reviewing the presentation in her mind. His presence had always unnerved her; she had forgotten that he'd be there this morning until this moment. He nodded at her as he made his way to the back of the room.

"Belinda, are you ready?" he asked.

"As ready as I'll ever be," she said. She regretted how it had sounded, so unsure of herself; it wasn't fair that the blond got her husband and her self-confidence all in one fell swoop.

"You'll be great," he assured her.

Mr. Whiting always undressed her with his eyes. Today was no different; she could feel his gaze peeling away the layers of her clothes.

Tall, broad-shouldered, with blond hair and piercing blue eyes, Robert Whiting was considered quite a catch. Belinda had entertained dirty thoughts about him a time or two, turned more than once to catch a glimpse of his backside as he passed. She always shook her head and reproached herself. She was a married woman; she didn't drool over men.

Today, though… she could drool all she wanted, over anyone that caught her eye. Mr. Whiting just happened to be foremost in her mind when it came to hot, single men. Belinda ran her hands down her waist and her round hips, feeling nervous. She checked her watch. Everyone else would be arriving shortly and she couldn't help but wonder if Mr. Whiting hadn't gotten here early just to get her alone.

In her mind's eye, she imagined sauntering towards him, returning that lustful gaze. Sliding down into his lap, feeling her skirt rise on her thighs. Exposing her garters and stockings, pressing herself against what she imagined was an impressive erection. She would lick her lips as she ran her hand slowly down the front of his pants, longing to unzip them so badly and wrap her dainty fingers around his manhood.

A loud sigh escaped her lips. She flushed, embarrassed. Perspiration teased the back of her neck; her blouse was damp. This was ridiculous, but she couldn't help it. She added this moment of embarrassment to her husband's lengthy list of crimes. Cut off from sex for a year, Belinda was so needy that she was ready to risk it all to bump and grind in the boardroom. More than that, Mr. Whiting was her boss, and far too young for her. She gave herself a sharp reprimand for her unacceptable behavior, pulling herself together.

If you like this sample, look for <u>**BBW Lost and Found- The Cruise Series, Book 1 by Jessica Johannsen**</u>.

Also by this Author:

<u>**Forgetting the Shared Wife**</u>

<u>**Double Whammy**</u>

<u>**Dexter's Renaissance**</u>

From the Author

If you enjoyed any of my books then please share the love and promote my books in Amazon.

If you write me a review and send me an email I will send you a free book, or many.
(Just know that these emails are filtered by my publisher.)

Good news is always welcome.

One Last Thing, For Kindle Readers...

When you turn the page, Kindle will give you the opportunity to rate this book and share your thoughts on Facebook and Twitter. If you enjoyed my writings, would you please take a few seconds to let your friends know about it? Because... when they enjoy they will be grateful to you and so will I.

Thank You!

Lee North
lee_north@awesomeauthors.org

About the Author

Born in 1940, Lee North is a Canadian who moved to Vancouver with his parents in 1950. His father was a newspaperman and artist. He married his high school sweetheart, and they are blessed with two sons, who then blessed them with four grandsons.

Lee North began his career in wholesale building materials. Ten years later, he got a job at a packaging manufacturer in Vancouver, selling paper and plastic. With hard work, he then became the General Manager. He retired in 2001.

In 2008, Lee North and his family moved to Comox Valley, their paradise valley. He loves traveling. During work years, he widely traveled in North America. And since 1995, through Europe and parts of Middle East.

"I took up writing ten years ago, as a hobby. I had a secret wish to be a writer and the free websites offered that opportunity. I try to confine my stories to locations that I have visited. The characters are fictional but can loosely be attached to people I have met along the way."